A Bold Claim

Jesse stirred, moaned, and reached for his head. He winced as his fingers found the bloody groove Slocum had laid on his temple.

"Damnation, that popskull you serve's powerful," Jesse James said. He sat up, held his head in both hands, and then looked up. For a second his eyes didn't focus. And then they did. He went for his six-shooter.

"Go on, Jesse," Slocum said, lounging back, both elbows resting on the bar. "It'll be real interesting to see if you can get your gun out before I can draw."

"Mister," the barkeep muttered. "He's a killer."

Over his shoulder, Slocum said, "He's not the only one. Might not even be the best killer in this room . . ."

JAKE LOGAN

SLOCUM AND THE JAMES GANG

JOVE BOOKS, NEW YORK

THE BERKLEY PUBLISHING GROUP
Published by the Penguin Group
Penguin Group (USA) Inc.
375 Hudson Street, New York, New York 10014, USA

Penguin Group (Canada), 90 Eglinton Avenue East, Suite 700, Toronto, Ontario M4P 2Y3, Canada
(a division of Pearson Penguin Canada Inc.)
Penguin Books Ltd., 80 Strand, London WC2R 0RL, England
Penguin Group Ireland, 25 St. Stephen's Green, Dublin 2, Ireland (a division of Penguin Books Ltd.)
Penguin Group (Australia), 250 Camberwell Road, Camberwell, Victoria 3124, Australia
(a division of Pearson Australia Group Pty. Ltd.)
Penguin Books India Pvt. Ltd., 11 Community Centre, Panchsheel Park, New Delhi—110 017, India
Penguin Group (NZ), 67 Apollo Drive, Rosedale, North Shore 0632, New Zealand
(a division of Pearson New Zealand Ltd.)
Penguin Books (South Africa) (Pty.) Ltd., 24 Sturdee Avenue, Rosebank, Johannesburg 2196,
South Africa

Penguin Books Ltd., Registered Offices: 80 Strand, London WC2R 0RL, England

This is a work of fiction. Names, characters, places, and incidents either are the product of the author's imagination or are used fictitiously, and any resemblance to actual persons, living or dead, business establishments, events, or locales is entirely coincidental.

SLOCUM AND THE JAMES GANG

A Jove Book / published by arrangement with the author

PRINTING HISTORY
Jove edition / December 2010

Copyright © 2010 by Penguin Group (USA) Inc.
Cover illustration by Sergio Giovine.

ISBN: 978-0-515-14871-8

JOVE®
Jove Books are published by The Berkley Publishing Group,
a division of Penguin Group (USA) Inc.
375 Hudson Street, New York, New York 10014.
JOVE® is a registered trademark of Penguin Group (USA) Inc.
The "J" design is a trademark of Penguin Group (USA) Inc.

PRINTED IN THE UNITED STATES OF AMERICA

10 9 8 7 6 5 4 3 2 1

1

"Mister, you just pistol-whipped Jesse James," the barkeep said.

"He deserved it," John Slocum said. He returned his Colt Navy to his holster, ignored the moaning outlaw on the sawdust-strewn barroom floor, and clicked his shot glass on the wood. When the bartender didn't stir, Slocum slammed it down hard. "Give me another one. And a pitcher of water."

"We already water down the whiskey," the barkeep muttered, but he poured Slocum the shot and rummaged about to get a large beer stein, which he filled with only slightly muddy water. He slid it across to Slocum, but his attention was on his fallen patron. He licked his lips and looked around as if judging the distance to the nearest window or door so he could escape as quick as possible.

Slocum knocked back the whiskey. It burned all the way down to his gullet and took away some of the dust he had accumulated on the trail getting to Las Vegas, New Mexico. He turned and stared at the stretched-out James. For two cents, he would have shot him rather than only laying the hard steel barrel alongside his head a couple times. Jesse

James had never done a damned thing for him and never would.

A hot, dry wind blew through the open door and decided Slocum. He picked up the stein of water, took a sip, and washed it around in his parched mouth. He considered spitting it on Jesse and then simply dumped the water over him. The water splashed off the outlaw's dirty face and caused soggy clumps to form in the sawdust on the barroom floor. Jesse stirred, moaned, and reached for his head. He winced as his fingers found the bloody groove Slocum had laid on his temple.

"Damnation, that popskull you serve's powerful," Jesse James said. He sat up, held his head in both hands, and then looked up. For a second his eyes didn't focus. And then they did. He went for his six-shooter.

"Go on, Jesse," Slocum said, lounging back, both elbows resting on the bar. "It'll be real interesting to see if you can get your gun out before I can draw."

"Mister," the barkeep muttered. "He's a *killer*."

Over his shoulder, Slocum said, "He's not the only one. Might not even be the best killer in this room." Since there were only the three of them in the saloon, it didn't take the barkeep long to understand what he was getting himself into. He backed off, finding the spot as far as possible from both Slocum and Jesse James. The painting of the reclining naked woman behind the bar was the only one looking down on the outlaw and his nemesis when the barkeep disappeared down a trapdoor.

"Slocum," the outlaw grated out. "You damned near busted my skull."

"It's too hard for that, Jesse." Slocum drained the few drops of water he hadn't already splattered on the outlaw, then set the heavy beer mug down on the bar. It wasn't likely now he'd have to use that on the outlaw's skull, too.

"You oughtta know. You tried bustin' it open 'fore, back in Lawrence. Right after the raid."

"You weren't there, Jesse, and you damn well know it. You were hardly sixteen."

"I was there," the outlaw insisted, getting to his feet. He leaned heavily against the bar. "You shot off your mouth about not likin' the way Quantrill wanted us to kill the little boys. I remember."

"You weren't there. I remember *that*."

"Well, I was at Centralia. Me and Bloody Bill was there and you weren't."

"No, I wasn't at that massacre," Slocum said. Old memories crowded in to bedevil him. He had protested Quantrill's murder of boys as young as eight years old in Lawrence, Kansas, and the guerrilla leader had told Bloody Bill Anderson to cut him down. And he had. Slocum had taken two slugs in the belly and was left to die in agony alongside the road leading away from the Kansas town.

Only he was tougher than that. He had survived, though it had taken long months to recover. By then Quantrill's Raiders had moved on to kill, rape, and maim throughout Kansas and into Missouri. But Jesse James had not been at the Lawrence raid, no matter how much he claimed to the contrary.

"See?" Jesse James said. His fingers came away red and sticky from the pistol-barrel-shaped groove in the side of his head. "Where's that barkeep?" He bellowed for him but the man was either hiding in his cellar or had figured out a way to clear out of town. Slocum was beginning to appreciate the man's point of view and thought it was about time for him to ride on, although he had just come in from a hard, dry ride from Santa Fe. The spring winds kicked up constant dust storms and his only traveling companions had been the occasional hundred-foot-tall dust devils spiraling their way across the desert.

Being alone with nothing but the taste of dust in his mouth for company seemed mighty good to him right now.

"Hey, Slocum, don't go. You just got here."

"Don't want to disturb you if you're on a serious drunk."

"Why'd you buffalo me like that? I was just gonna buy you a drink. Hell, let me do that right now." The outlaw went around the bar, found a bottle, and poured two shots of whiskey. "This might be the good stuff and not that trade whiskey the barkeep was foistin' off on me." He tossed back the shot, made a face, then poured himself another. "Yup, this is the good stuff. I can't hardly taste the rusty nails or the gunpowder in it." He held it up and squinted at the label. "Ain't never been within five hundred miles of Kaintucky, though."

"You're a ways from Clay County," Slocum said. He didn't have that much of a quarrel with Jesse but felt he had owed him for being such good friends with Bloody Bill. As he had recuperated, first in Kansas and later back at Slocum's Stand in Calhoun, Georgia, he had followed the newspaper reports and had grown angrier every time he finished reading. War was war but what they did amounted to cruelty for the sake of inflicting misery.

Killing a man because he wore a Federal uniform and wanted to drive his bayonet through your guts was a world away from riding into a town filled with civilians, a dozen six-guns hanging from your bandoliers, and emptying first one and then the next pistol at anything that moved. Even the Centralia Massacre had been brutal, injured Federal soldiers slaughtered as they lay in a field hospital.

"I am surely that, Slocum." Jesse James leaned over the bar and whispered conspiratorially. "You want in on a sure thing? A man like you, real smart and good with a gun, you can be something special."

"I am in on a sure thing," Slocum said. "The sun comes up every morning and the stars come out at night."

"Damnation, you always were a philosopher."

"How would you know? We weren't together that long."

"But we did ride together. Gunpowder and blood shared and spilled. Those make us brothers, Slocum."

"My brother died at Gettysburg."

"Do tell. Damn Yankees."

"Damned Pickett. He was a fool for making his attack into the muzzles and bores of so many bluecoats."

"George Pickett wasn't so outstanding," Jesse James said, "but we had some of the finest generals. Not even the fightingest men and cleverest generals amounted to a bucket of warm shit because the Yanks wore us down, Slocum. They didn't have anybody as good as Longstreet or Jackson or Early or good ole' Robert E. himself."

"At least you didn't include Quantrill."

"He was a Northerner," Jesse James said without any animosity. "You got to admit he gave his own side a run for their money, but he was an Ohio boy born and bred."

Slocum poured himself another drink since it wasn't likely for the bartender to keep track of what was owed. He was tuckered out from the trail and knew he had quite a few miles ahead of him if he wanted to get through Raton Pass and into Colorado. Nothing waited for him there, but it wasn't Las Vegas—and Jesse James wasn't there, wherever there might be at the end of the trail.

"You on the run?" Slocum asked. He was beginning to wish a mirror hung behind the bar rather than the garish picture of a voluptuous woman. The hair on the back of his neck prickled up as he wondered if the town marshal was likely to come in with shotgun blazing. More likely, if the lawman had a lick of sense, he would surround the saloon and set fire to it, then let a dozen deputies shoot anything that came scurrying out.

"Well, sir, not exactly," Jesse said, looking as thoughtful as he was likely to. "That's why I wanted to enlist your aid."

"What is it? Train? Bank? Las Vegas doesn't have a bank worth the mention."

"I saw it on the way in," Jesse said, "and you got quite the eye for that, Slocum. If there's a thousand dollars in the vault—ever—it'd surprise the hell out of me." He leaned forward and whispered so low Slocum could hardly hear. "This is bigger. A lot bigger."

"Do tell. I have places to be," Slocum said. "Thanks for the drink."

"Wait, Slocum. You're the kind of man I need. I mean it. This is *big*."

Slocum hesitated. The James Gang was wanted by every sheriff and marshal from here all the way to the Mississippi— and even on the eastern side. Tales of their robberies were little more than campfire boasts, if Slocum was a judge, but there wasn't any doubt Jesse had been successful and had gotten away with more than his share of loot. If anyone could be called an outlaw pioneer, it was him and his brother Frank. Before they had put their mind to it, nobody robbed trains and their rolling bank vaults carrying payrolls and other valuables from one city to another.

"Got your attention, I see," Jesse James said, grinning. He was the sort of man who ought to be selling snake oil. His manner was slick and his words sounded so truthful. Slocum had to tell himself this was the same man who had slaughtered innocent civilians during the war.

He snorted. So had he, but the difference was great. He hadn't liked it and he had stopped. He put his hand on his belly where the two bullets had ripped through his flesh. The scars went deeper than his skin. Those slugs had turned him around and put him on a different path, not that he hadn't robbed a bank or stagecoach in his day. Compared to Jesse James, though, he was an amateur.

"How much gold you want, Slocum? A fistful of double eagles? More bullion than your horse can carry? More than a damned pack train of mules can carry?"

"Nobody in New Mexico has that kind of gold," Slocum said. "Not even the garrison over at Fort Union calls up a payroll that big."

Jesse moved away slightly at the mention of the cavalry outpost.

"No, they don't have money like that."

"You need to be a hell of a lot more specific to get my attention." Slocum eyed the bottle. Only a few drinks had been taken from it, and it was good whiskey. His mouth was still cottony and the aches and pains from being in the saddle for weeks yearned to be dulled with the alcohol.

He poured himself another. Jesse James took this as a good sign.

"You're still quite a thinker, Slocum. Always one step ahead. You won't regret what's in store for you."

"Tell me."

"You've heard of the Knights of the Golden Circle," Jesse started. He reared back and his hand flashed to his six-shooter as galloping horses outside caught his attention.

Slocum looked over his shoulder and saw familiar faces enter. He recognized Frank James and another of the gang who was always bad news. Charlie Dennison was as cold-blooded a killer that ever sat astride a horse. He swung a sawed-off shotgun around when he saw Slocum.

"Wait, Charlie, don't. Get your fingers off them triggers," Jesse ordered. "Me and Slocum, we're discussing some important matters."

"Talk somewhere else, Jesse," Frank said. "We got the law on our tracks."

"The train," Jesse said. "I told you boys not to bother, that we got bigger fish to fry."

"It was so damned easy, Jesse," Frank said. "The grade almost caused the boiler to explode as the engine struggled up into Apache Pass. We jumped down off real high rocks on either side, got into the mail car, and it didn't take a minute to get the clerk to open it up."

"You kill him?" Slocum asked.

"You're still the lily-livered coward you ever was, Slocum," Charlie Dennison said. He started to lift his room-sweeper again, but Frank James forced the barrels down.

"You heard Jesse. Slocum—"

"How much did you take?" Jesse became more animated than before and color came to his cheeks. His breathing was faster and his eyes sparkled. Slocum recognized the emotions. He had felt them himself right after a robbery, anticipating what the take might have been but before seeing how little there really was to go around a goodly-sized gang.

"Not so much. Maybe five hunnerd dollars," Dennison said. "But it was easy."

"You didn't think the mail clerk could identify you if you killed him. Ever consider wearing masks?"

"Slocum, you—"

"Shut up, Charlie. We got to go, Jesse. Now. That posse can't be a half hour behind us."

"They're here!" came the shout from outside. If the lookout said anything more, Slocum couldn't hear for the fusillade that made his ears ring. The last time he had heard so many guns firing all at once had been in battle during the war.

Two more of the gang shoved through the swinging doors, their rifles firing out into the street. The glass windows exploded as the posse opened fire, not caring what they shot at or what they hit.

"Can't get out this way," Jesse called, peering through the back door. "They got the whole damned place surrounded."

Slocum had the cartridges in his Colt and maybe a dozen more rounds. He doubted any of the gang had more ammunition than he did. That didn't make for a long standoff.

He cursed under his breath. Just being in the same room as Jesse James was enough for any lawman to drop a noose around his neck, too. It didn't matter that he hadn't committed the train robbery. Slocum fired twice as an incautious posse member thought to look inside. He might have winged the man but doubted it. There wasn't the gut feeling he got when he knew a round had found its target. He wasn't as inclined to kill any of the posse since that would only infuriate the ones remaining and maybe let them recruit more from the local townspeople.

"What are we going to do, Jesse?" Frank fired steadily. From the sounds outside, his aim was better than it had any right to be. But even as Slocum hoped they might drive away the posse for a few minutes, he heard Frank's rifle come up empty. When he reached for his six-shooter, that signaled how dire their predicament was.

Charlie Dennison fired repeatedly using his shotgun, but Slocum saw he was running out of shells as his coat pocket looked more and more starved.

They were running out of time to stay alive.

Slocum vaulted the bar, landed hard, and went to his knees.

"Yeah, Slocum, hide," called Dennison. "I didn't expect any more than that from you."

Slocum found the trapdoor the barkeep had used to escape and yanked it open. A ladder went down but he didn't bother. He jumped down and found himself in a dimly lit cellar. Kegs of beer stayed cool underground, but only a couple cases of whiskey were stored here. Slocum had to walk slightly hunched over since his six-foot frame wasn't built for the low ceiling, but it didn't take an expert tracker to follow the barkeep's footprints out. The man had pissed himself and left muddy tracks.

The far side of the cellar had another trapdoor in the ceiling. Slocum pushed it up and peered around an abandoned building that might have been a bakery at one time. With a surge, he threw back the trapdoor and pulled himself up.

The rest of the gang followed closely.

"There're our horses," Frank James said, pointing out the front door. "How are we going to get to 'em?"

"Walk," Slocum said. "Put your guns away. Don't run. Just saunter on over, mount, and ride."

"You boys know where we're gonna rendezvous," Jesse said. "Slocum, we're meeting at—"

Slocum didn't hear him. He was already out the door

and squinting into the bright spring sun. Forcing himself to follow his own advice was hard. Jumping into the saddle and riding like the demons of hell were nipping at his spurs was quite a lure. He passed one man wearing a deputy's star pinned on his vest and grabbed him by the shoulder. He shoved him toward the saloon.

"Get in there," Slocum shouted. "You don't want them to get away, do you?"

"No, but they got shotguns and—"

"Move!" Not for nothing had Slocum been a captain in the C.S.A. His voice carried the sharp edge of command. The deputy ran to the swinging doors as if he'd sat down on a hill of red ants.

Slocum got to his horse, swung into the saddle, and turned. The entire posse had rushed into the saloon and were shouting at each other, wondering where their quarry had gotten off to. The getaway would have gone smoother if Charlie Dennison hadn't let out a rebel yell, ridden up on the boardwalk, and started shooting through the shattered windows at the lawmen inside.

Putting his heels to his horse's flanks, Slocum rocketed away. He was creating quite a stir because the local citizens were peering out from drawn-back curtains and through barely opened doors to see what was going on. This much gunfire convinced even the bravest man it was time to go to earth and wait out the hail of bullets.

As Slocum passed the gunsmith's store, he saw a rifle poke out. He ducked as the smith fired at him. The heavy slug harmlessly ripped past his head. Slocum used his spurs now to convince his horse that galloping was the only gait out of Las Vegas.

Behind him, he heard the others in the gang laughing, boasting, shouting insults as they left.

"This way, Slocum. Come on. Ride with us or they'll catch you for certain sure!"

Slocum ignored Jesse James and cut off the road, heading westward for the Sangre de Cristo Mountains, where he could find some shelter until the posse's fervor cooled down.

He hadn't ridden a mile when he realized the posse had ignored Jesse and followed only one rider—him. Slocum rode faster, but his mare tired quickly. Reaching the mountains would be more than a chore. It'd be impossible.

2

There wasn't any way in hell Slocum could reach the mountains and find sanctuary there. A quick glance to his right showed that the southern way was out of the question. It was open desert, cut through with arroyos that might provide a little cover—but so what? The posse was hot on his trail. All of them. Somehow, they had lost Jesse James's trail and had come pounding along after him.

Slocum took a quick glance to the north, hoping the terrain would be different. It was rocky desert also, but had a few ridges running through it where he might duck down out of sight. If any of the lawmen following him was a tracker, he was a goner. If he'd had an hour or two head start, he could have hidden his trail, but they were almost on top of him. His horse was tired from the ride up from Santa Fe and badly needed some water. For all that, Slocum could do with more than a sip of something liquid that wasn't whiskey. The rotgut he had swilled in the bar tore away at his insides. It had gone down his gullet just fine back in town but now it was almost torture enduring the way it burned at his belly.

If he didn't think of something soon, that might be the last taste of liquor he'd ever get. The posse seemed inclined to turn into a lynch mob from the way they hooted and hollered behind him.

He dropped down into an arroyo that slanted toward the northwest and safety in the mountains. This wouldn't fool them long. Slocum wanted to buy a minute here and a second there with his little tricks. Staying ahead of them was the only way he was going to stay alive.

Gunshots rang out behind him, but he knew he was still too distant for the men to get a good shot. They wanted to spook him, nothing more. Slocum had been in tight spots before and wasn't going to be herded like some damned sheep. But the way his belly groaned and protested all the whiskey he had drunk!

Every bounce of the horse caused another drop or two of the acid inside him to splash up. When some came to his mouth, he wanted to puke. Holding it back was the best he could do. There wasn't time to get rid of the foul load he carried inside, and if he did, he would mark his trail as surely as if he had painted red arrows on the rocks all around showing which way he had ridden.

"We got 'im, boys. We trapped ourselves a member of the infamous James Gang!"

Slocum maneuvered his way up the sandy-bottomed ravine, climbed up to the far rim when he found a part of the embankment that had collapsed under its own weight, and kept moving steadily for the mountains. Among the trees and rocky stretches, he could lose a posse a hundred times as big. But he had to reach higher ground first. This stretch of the desert sported only low-growing shrubs with occasional scrub oak that was so stunted it barely grew chest-high. He wove in and out through the increasingly tall piñon pines and slowly left the ruckus raised by the posse behind. They might have taken a wrong fork or they might simply be tiring.

Slocum felt half past dead but kept riding. His life depended on it.

"Damn you, Jesse," he muttered. "You always were bad luck."

He had ridden with Jesse and his brother Frank only a couple times before the Lawrence raid—and no matter what lies Jesse James told, he hadn't been there. Every man's face on that raid was etched in his brain. He knew the ones that had gotten excited when they began killing small boys and even a woman or two. And he remembered the others who, like him, had ridden through the sleepy Kansas town with grim expressions etched on stony faces. They were the soldiers following orders and took no pleasure from the killing.

Bloody Bill Anderson's laughter as he gunned down anything that moved still rang in Slocum's ears. The image of William Quantrill's face, eyes bright and expression fixed hypnotically on each of his victims, was even worse. Slocum's hand moved to the two bullet scars on his belly.

He almost lost the liquor again as he traced across those circular pink scars. Forgetting the men on that raid was impossible. Jesse James hadn't been among their number.

Slocum was ashamed after all these years that he had been.

Sounds from behind told him the posse had found his tracks leading out of the arroyo. He made for a stand of pines, hoping to get out of sight. For a moment he thought he had succeeded and then a slug ripped away part of a tree trunk a few feet away and spattered him with sap. He recoiled, jerked his horse in the opposite direction, and quickly found it was too late to change his path. The lawmen were on two sides, cutting off escape. He urged his horse up a game trail, through the woods, and finally into the foothills, where huge boulders were strewn about as if a careless giant child had dropped them after tiring of such stony toys.

He wedged himself between two and kept going up the

increasingly steep trail until he came out into a clearing. His heart sank. The posse was too close for him to get to the far side without being seen. His only hope of getting out of this alive was to make a stand at the rocky passage. He could hold off the entire posse until his ammo ran out.

He wished he had a couple sticks of dynamite. Blowing up the trail would bring an avalanche down, sealing the way. Slocum might as well have wished for a mountain howitzer.

Wheeling his horse about, he dragged out his Winchester and levered in a round. The best chance he had was of wounding a few of the posse and scaring them off. If he accidentally killed one, they'd have blood in their eye and never give up the chase. He was a good shot—one of the best—but firing down such a narrow passageway would cause unpredictable ricochets. He was as likely to blow off a man's head as his hat.

"Up here!"

Slocum swiveled at the waist, bringing the stock to his shoulder and sighting high up into the rocks to his right. His finger stopped halfway from firing when he saw a woman waving at him.

"Come on up, and be quick about it. You don't have much time 'fore they get through that gap. The trail's over there." She pointed. For a moment, Slocum didn't see what she meant. Then he saw a tiny dirt patch that vanished into rocks. He wouldn't be able to ride such a narrow trail. He swung his leg over and dropped to the ground, yanking on the reins to get his mare moving behind him. He clung to his rifle in the other hand, fearing the posse would burst through at any instant.

"They're scared to come after you because that would turn into such a duck blind," she called down. "But they won't wait forever. There's a deputy sheriff egging them on."

The trail was hardly the width of Slocum's boots, but it was wide enough. He hurried up, pulling his reluctant horse behind. The horse's flanks rubbed against rock, first on one side and then the other, but the drop wasn't too great and he eventually came out on top where the woman had built a small campfire. A pot of coffee sat beside the fire.

"Get your horse unsaddled and rubbed down as quick as you can. And keep your mouth shut." She shoved the ceramic coffeepot into the fire so that it came to a boil within a minute. The fragrant odor curled up and made Slocum's nose wrinkle and belly turn somersaults.

"They'll smell it," he said. He dumped his saddle to the ground next to the woman's, then spread his blanket so it caught some of the afternoon sun to dry. His horse had lathered up from the chase followed by such a steep climb.

"I told you to shut up," she said. She began breaking open boxes and unwrapping parcels wound with oilskin, preparing a decent enough meal of dried meat and bread so hard it could be used to drive nails. Along with it were jars of mustard and relish, or maybe it was preserves. From where Slocum rubbed down his horse, he couldn't tell.

The smell of the boiling coffee grew stronger. Below he heard the excited cries of the posse as they finally summoned up the nerve to come through the narrow crevice in the rocks.

"Quiet," she cautioned when he started to speak.

He kept wiping off the flecks of lather but got a chance to study the woman more closely. At first he had thought she was older than he was, but that came from a heavy layer of trail dust on her face. She might have been in her mid-twenties. From the strands of unruly hair poking out from under her wide-brimmed hat, she was a brunette, although her hair might have been auburn and completely caked with dirt. She wore men's britches but a decidedly womanly blouse that might have been fine linen. Like everything else about her, it hadn't been cleaned in weeks. Expensive boots on her feet hinted at money the rest of her outfit didn't bespeak.

What interested Slocum most was the shiny patch on her

jeans at the right hip, as if she rode with a holster rubbing the cloth smooth. Where the six-shooter might have been placed, he couldn't tell. As she turned, he saw more evidence that she usually wore a hogleg. She turned and was slightly off-balance, as if compensating for the lack of three pounds of iron at her side.

"What are you looking at, mister?" Her lips thinned and she tried to look hard at him. He laughed. She didn't do a very good job of appearing stern.

"My savior," he said. "Never thought you'd be this pretty either." He wasn't blowing smoke when he said this. Her finely boned face might have been filthy but he saw the beauty there. She was slender and had quite a shape under the ill-fitting clothing. The blouse was far too big for her and the jeans were far too tight. Slocum only objected to the blouse.

She saw him staring at her and self-consciously checked to be sure the buttons were fastened all the way up to her chin. Slocum held back a broad grin because he didn't dare make the woman angry at him when she was going out of her way to make it look as if the two of them had camped here all night long.

Slocum ducked under his horse and rolled so he came up on his blanket. He dropped his head down to his saddle and pulled his hat low to make it look as if he was asleep. He wished he'd had time to change his shirt because he was certain the posse had gotten a good look at him somewhere during the chase.

"Howdy," the woman called, holding up an empty tin cup to her lips. She made a smacking sound and dropped the cup to the edge of the fire. "You gents want some coffee? Just fixed up a fresh batch since we drank the first."

Four of the posse crowded up the trail.

"You been up here long?"

"Yup," she said. "Me and my man, we been here all night."

"How come?" The man wearing the deputy sheriff's badge edged closer, his hand resting on his six-shooter.

"Truth is, this oaf got us lost. He can't read a map for love nor money. And after stranding us out here all night, he's not getting much of either."

"You see a rider?"

"Seen lots of 'em," she said. "You want some coffee, you'll have to use your own cups. All we got's two, one for each of us." She poured some of the witch's brew she had boiled into the cup. It poured like mud.

"Fact is, the gent we're after looks a powerful lot like him." The deputy threw down and got his six-gun from his holster in a respectable move. He pointed the muzzle straight at Slocum.

"What'd you go and wake me up for?" Slocum said, rubbing his eyes. He turned from the deputy as if he didn't have a six-gun leveled at him and asked, "That acid you call coffee ready to drink?"

"It's only fit drinking for a human being. That leaves you out." She looked at the deputy and said, "Put that thing down, unless it's a crime not to be able to read a map. If it is, then you take him into custody. He's one piss poor guide."

"Guide?"

"I hired him up in Denver to get us to Taos. How close are we to Taos?"

"Fifty miles," the deputy said, not sure what to make of the situation.

"Fifty! I told you I had to be there by the tenth of the month. There's a wedding. The Armijos' daughter is getting hitched, and I'm in the wedding party. You know her? Consuelo Armijo?"

"I know Provencio Armijo. He's 'bout the richest man in Taos. Owns three stores and the livery," piped up the man behind the deputy.

"That's not half of what he owns. Consuelo and me went

to boarding school back East. You ever hear of Kecksburg, Pennsylvania? She and I—"

"He's been with you all night?"

"All night and for the past week," she said with just the proper amount of disgust in her voice. Slocum saw the subtle shift in her expression as she watched the deputy closely. She knew she had carried off the lie. "Now, as I was saying, Consuelo and I—"

"Taos is in that direction," the deputy said, using his six-shooter to point westward. "You bust your hump and you might make it 'fore the tenth. Today's the sixth."

"I ought to be there early, for the wedding rehearsal," the woman said. She took off her hat and let long strands of auburn hair cascade down. She ran her fingers through it and got some of the caked mud free. "I'll need a day to get all cleaned up, too."

"You didn't see another rider?"

"We been on the trail until we got lost a day back. Of course we've seen other riders."

"I mean today. In the past hour." The deputy looked around and everything appeared to be as the woman said. Slocum held his breath. If any of the posse checked his horse, they'd see he'd only had time to rub down the side facing them. The far side was still lathered up.

She saw how the deputy was looking at Slocum's horse so she stood, turned, and pointed back down the trail. "I thought I saw a rider not fifteen minutes before you came up the trail. He was riding like his horse's tail was on fire, making for the far side of that clearing. If he kept going the way he did, he'd be in Taos by now."

"Taos is in the other direction," Slocum said.

"No it ain't," the deputy said, glaring at Slocum. "What kind of trailsman are you? The lady's right. Taos is that way."

"Well, thank you, Marshal. At last a man who knows how to find his way in this wilderness."

"Deputy sheriff, ma'am," he said. But Slocum saw the man's attention had been diverted from the horse to the stretch between the rocky gap and the far side of the clearing. "Git on along, you mangy cayuses," the lawman said to his posse. "Turn 'round and head back down the trail."

"Ain't no trail. That's hardly more 'n a footpath."

Slocum caught his breath. The last man to come up frowned, as if trying to think of something important.

"Been a rider on the trail recently," he said.

"Of course there has been. You, silly," the woman said.

"No, I mean somebody else. I seen signs of—"

"Three other riders," she finished for him. "You brought up the rear. The marshal and his other two deputies were ahead of you, so of course you saw tracks."

"No, I mean there was—"

"It's deputy sheriff, ma'am. Shut yer tater trap, Benny, and head back down. We got ourselves an outlaw to catch."

The woman started to speak, but Slocum caught her eye. She was going to ask what the outlaw had done. That was a natural question, but if she asked, the deputy would answer and prolong the time in camp. Eventually one of them would twig to Slocum's recent arrival. The fourth man in the posse almost had. Slocum wasn't sure what he had seen along the trail, but it should have been conclusive evidence everything wasn't as it appeared in camp.

"You folks have a good trip to Taos."

"If you're heading in that direction, Marshal—I mean Sheriff," she said easily, pretending to make the same mistake repeatedly. "You drop on by the wedding reception. It's going to be a jim-dandy one. The Armijos are known for the parties they throw, and this is a special one, even bigger than Consuelo's *quinceaños* festival."

The deputy let out a low whistle.

"I heard of some of them parties lasting a week or more, almost 'til the girl's sixteen!"

With thoughts of free food and booze flowing like water,

the four men retraced their way to the rocky gap, where they joined three others before riding hard across the clearing.

Slocum waited until the dust had settled and the posse was out of sight.

"I'm much obliged," he said.

"For what?" she asked.

"Not that coffee. You could have poisoned them all to death, or was that the idea?"

She stared at him, then burst out laughing.

"You're not what I expected at all."

"You make it sound as if you knew I'd be hightailing it through the crevice a couple minutes ahead of a posse."

She brushed back her hair and came to sit beside him. She pressed close, her breasts against his arm. Slocum wasn't inclined to move away, not with her face only inches from his.

"What's your name?" he asked.

"What's it matter?" She kissed him. Hard.

3

Slocum started to pull back and then found the kiss softening—and he didn't mind it one bit. The woman pressed even closer and carried him back to the blanket, lying half atop him. Only then did she pull back and look down at him. Her brown eyes were flecked with gold highlights, and sparkled with . . . what? Slocum couldn't tell.

"You sure pulled my fat out of the fire," he said. "Thanks for that."

"I saw you were in trouble."

"You always go siding with whoever the posse is chasing?"

She laughed, and it was a delighted, delightful sound. She reached out and put a long-fingered hand on his cheek. Her touch was both soft and exciting.

"Don't do much riding, do you?" he asked, trying to figure her out.

"What makes you say that?" She pulled back a little and looked hard at him.

"The calluses on your hands."

"What calluses?" She looked at the hand that had so recently stroked over his stubbled cheek.

22

"That's the point," Slocum said, enjoying the small flare of anger he saw. Her cheeks turned rosy and the way her mouth turned gave her fine face even more definition as muscles tightened and dimples formed.

"You're a lot smarter than I thought," she finally said, settling back down next to him.

"You don't know me," he said, "so how can I be smarter—or dumber—than you expected? I didn't know I was going to ride this way until I ran into a touch of trouble back in Las Vegas."

"Where'd the rest of the gang go? Do you have a secret meeting place? A hideout nearby?"

"I'm not a member of the James Gang," Slocum said. "I didn't know Jesse was even in town until I saw him knocking back shots of whiskey in that saloon."

"You weren't meeting up with him?"

"I pistol-whipped him." This caused a reaction. Her eyes widened, but she said nothing. "I owed him. He could have spoken up for me and didn't." It was only his imagination but the two scars from the bullets Bloody Bill had put in him itched. "Don't rightly know if he enjoyed the sight of me kicking on the floor and bleeding to death."

"That's not his reputation. He's something of a hero."

Slocum snorted.

"Some hero. He steals from the rich because they have the money. What money he gives to anyone poorer than him is because he is buying their silence. Without a whale of a lot of closed mouths, the law would have caught him a long time back."

"I thought you were one of the gang. I was wrong."

"I don't know if I'd gun him down, but if that happened, I wouldn't lose much sleep over it. Some of the men riding with Jesse are worse than he is. Killing them wouldn't be a chore at all, it'd be a public service."

"So you hope the deputy sheriff finds the gang?"

Slocum didn't answer right away. Things had happened

too quick for him to consider what it all meant. Jesse and the others had likely ridden off without a care in the world because the entire posse had come after him. Jesse James wouldn't care if Slocum got his neck stretched and he certainly wouldn't spend a minute's time thinking on whether to break him out of jail if the deputy had dragged him back to Las Vegas as a prisoner.

"Doesn't matter to me one way or the other," Slocum said. That summed up what he thought fairly well. "All I want is to ride north."

"What's up there for you?"

"Nothing more than what's waiting for me here," Slocum said. The woman had snuggled even closer when he told her his interest in the James Gang wasn't all that great one way or the other. He kissed her again.

"Hmmm, nice," she said, moving against him like a cat, making sinuous wiggling motions so she could wrap her legs around his thigh. She began rocking up and down until Slocum thought she would purr.

He reached down and popped open the top button. She made no move to stop him. He opened a couple more and revealed the creamy swell of her breasts. The blouse had been loose and hid her ample charms. When he got the rest of the buttons open, she shrugged her shoulders and shucked off the unwanted garment, leaving her naked to the waist.

"My turn," she said as she began working to pull off his gun belt and then the buttons on his fly. "Oh, my."

Slocum heaved a sigh of relief as she worked free the last button and let his hardness leap out. It had been getting mighty tight at the crotch. But the relief was quickly replaced with other sensations as she took him in her mouth and began kissing and licking his meaty shaft.

Leaning back, Slocum stared up into the sky and watched clouds swirl and build, mimicking what he was experiencing down lower. He thought of her tongue working on him the way the wind built clouds up into thunder heads.

And then he reached down and pulled her away.

"What? You don't like it?"

"I'm greedy," he said. "I want more."

"More?" She drew back from him and got to her knees. The warm sunlight turned her naked, snowy breasts into glowing, vibrant mounds he wanted to sample. But she pushed him back, got to her feet, and began stripping off her jeans. Slocum found himself appreciating the sight of her shedding the tight pants the way a snake molted. Her wiggles and shakes caused her breasts to bob about in a motion that made Slocum even harder simply from watching.

When she stepped out of the jeans to stand buck naked, he found himself struggling to keep from showing exactly how much he was aroused by the sight.

She stepped across his body, giving him a view far better than watching clouds. The furry thatch between her legs was dotted with tiny dewdrops betraying her arousal. Slowly, she settled down so her knees pressed in on either side of his body, and her legs parted delightfully above his groin. Slocum gasped as she fully lowered down over him, taking him into her heated core. When she reached around and began stroking his balls, Slocum fought to keep from behaving like a young buck with his first woman.

"You surely do know how to get down to the essentials," he said.

"I'm inspired," she said, twisting her hips slightly so he stirred about inside her. She closed her eyes and a look of desire came to her face. Slocum reached up and took her tits, toying with the hard nubs capping each. The nipples pulsed and throbbed with every frenzied beat of her heart.

He pressed down, crushing them almost flat. As if this wasn't enough for her, she leaned forward so he pressed into them with even more power. Then she began bending forward to lift herself off his shaft. Slocum abandoned his posts and stroked along her body, holding her waist and then reaching behind to grab two delightful handfuls of ass flesh.

"Oh, yes," she said as he pulled her back down around him.

They worked together, his hands guiding her and her inner muscles massaging and gripping at him like a hand in a velvet glove. Heat mounted inside him and turned into a fire that threatened to burn him up. He began stroking and pulling the doughy half-moons apart and then pressing them together as she moved up and down with increasing speed. Friction mounted and Slocum felt his control slipping away. He held back as long as he could and the woman cried out. Her body shook uncontrollably and then her hips went wild.

She rose and dropped with increasing speed, with increasing need, until Slocum exploded. This set her off again so that she trembled like a leaf in a high wind. Then she bent forward, thrust her legs backward on either side of Slocum's, and lay fully atop him. She put her sweaty cheek against his chest.

"Your heart's still racing," she said, positioning her ear just above the hammering organ.

"Can't imagine why," Slocum said. He stroked down the sleek back and along her womanly curves.

"Audrey Underwood," she said.

"John Slocum."

He had to laugh. It had taken them all this time to get around to names.

"What's funny?"

"We could have been in a powerful lot of trouble if the deputy had asked me what your name was," he said.

"And asked me what yours was," Audrey said. She laughed now, too. Slocum liked the musical sound of her voice and merriment almost as much as he had the soft moans of her passion.

"We could have lied," Slocum said.

"You do that often, John?"

"Only when I want to or have to."

"You're lying now. I'm a good judge of men. You aren't

a liar. You'd sooner cut out your own tongue than go against your word."

"That why you stripped down and made love with me?"

"I said I was a good judge of when men are telling the truth. I'm not such a good judge of men when it comes to a roll in the hay." The tinge of bitterness to her words told him of a string of broken hearts.

"You could always get to know a man before bedding him."

"Would you have preferred that?"

"No."

"See? I pegged you right. You tell the truth. And you say you're not one of Jesse James's gang?"

"Never was, see no reason ever to ride that trail with him."

"You really pistol-whipped him?"

"More like buffaloed. I only hit him once or twice. That was all it took to knock him out."

"Men have died for less," Audrey said. She looked at him strangely, then said, "You're not lying about this either. I'm amazed."

"No need to lie. I've known Jesse since he was a whippersnapper." Slocum wondered if that were true. He'd known Jesse since he was sixteen and even then he was a killer with a bent toward doing things illegally even if walking the straight and narrow path was easier. Some men were naturally inclined to be crooks and killers. Jesse James was one of those.

Audrey fell silent, then stood and began dressing. Slocum enjoyed this sight almost as much as when she had taken off the blouse and jeans. Getting into the tight pants was the part he liked best. Then he knew he had to be moving on. He had no idea why Audrey had spoken up for him the way she had or what brought her to the foothills of the Sangre de Cristo Mountains, but whatever it was didn't involve him. He buttoned himself up and settled his gun belt around his waist until it felt right.

"You a shootist?" she asked.

"Don't think of myself that way. I've wrangled cattle and done a bit of gambling."

"And killing?"

"That, too, but usually when the owlhoot deserved it. Sometimes not, maybe, but I always had a good reason at the time."

"Jesse'd say the same thing."

"Reckon you're right. Much obliged for the way you spoke up for me in front of the deputy and his men." Slocum hesitated and looked at Audrey Underwood.

"Yes, John? What is it?"

"You need to learn to make better coffee. Drinking that swill is a sure road to a cemetery."

She looked surprised, then laughed. As she shook her head, her hair floated around her dirty face, giving her an auburn halo shot with strands of gold to match her eyes.

"I need your help."

"Doing what?"

"I'm after Jesse James."

"You a bounty hunter?" The notion struck him as ridiculous, but Audrey didn't deny it. "Bounty hunters can't hesitate to kill their quarry. You up for that?"

"I could shoot Jesse James," she said. "But bringing him back isn't exactly what I'm after."

"What are you after, then?"

"Jesse stole a passel of money back in Kansas, and it was never found. He might have brought it out here with him."

"More likely he spent it on whores and whiskey," Slocum said.

"He didn't. He brought it with him. A lot of gold. Maybe as much as ten thousand dollars."

"So you're looking to find where he hid the gold and collect a reward?" Slocum's ideas turned to something else. Any reward would be a fraction of the value. Better to find the gold and ride off with it. Stealing from a road agent wasn't exactly stealing, after all. And who threw their brand on a sack of gold coins? They could belong to anyone who claimed it.

"Something like that. My employer put me on to this and then wouldn't back me coming here. I intend to prove him wrong and write the best danged article any reporter ever submitted to the *Kansas City Star Gazette*."

"You'd do better to forget the treasure hunt and just write a story about his victims."

"He's out here to spend that money, to use it for something even more vile than whores and whiskey."

"What's that?"

"I . . . I don't know. But I'm going to find out. and you'll help, won't you, John? We can be partners. I'll even give you a byline, but your name'd be second, of course, since this is my story."

"I don't cotton much to having my name bandied about in a newspaper."

"You could be famous. *We* could be famous if this story is as big as I think. There wasn't any call for Jesse to leave Kansas. The federal marshal there lost his trail in a rainstorm and gave up hunting for him. All Jesse had to do was to fade into the countryside, let his family and friends hide him for a spell, then find a new train to rob."

"How'd this posse get on his trail? They mistook me for one of his gang."

"Jesse has been laying low but Frank sees New Mexico as an apple to be plucked as they ride past the tree. The two of them have been feuding. Not much, mind you, but there have been arguments and I caught wind of it. That's how I found them."

"Found them?" Slocum snorted. If Jesse James wanted to disappear, Audrey Underwood wouldn't have a ghost of a chance finding him. Jesse was strutting around in public for a reason—and that was simple enough. The law out here in New Mexico Territory wasn't hunting him for a string of train and bank robberies. Until brother Frank had stirred them up, that is.

"Scoff if you will, but I tracked them here. Somewhere in these hills lies the secret reason Jesse came to New Mexico and I intend to find what it is."

"With my help?" Slocum thought hard on the idea that Jesse had brought that much gold with him. There had always been an unpredictable streak in the outlaw. Sometimes that boiled over to him gunning down a man for no good reason—or a reason only Jesse understood. But one thing had been a constant in Jesse's life and that was a real yen for gold. He was like a bloodhound on a scent when he went after a train shipment. If he had brought some spoils from a robbery or two with him, Jesse would have hidden it where only he could find it.

It would be a waste to let a crook like Jesse James have all that gold for himself.

"What do you want me to do?"

"They know you. You . . . you could ride with them and get clues."

"After swatting Jesse alongside the head with my pistol barrel, he's not likely to confide such things in me." Slocum listened to Audrey ramble on with a dozen lame reasons why he would fit right in, but only one occurred to him—and she had no way of knowing it. Why had Jesse extended his hand in friendship to get Slocum to ride with the gang? He had started to explain why he and the rest of his cutthroats had ridden into the territory when the deputy sheriff had shown up with his posse.

Jesse had wanted something from Slocum and had been on the brink of asking when their discussion had been busted up.

"Might not be too hard getting in with him," Slocum said as if thinking aloud. "What's in it for me?"

Audrey smiled broadly, showing her dimples.

"There's nothing that says all the gold has to be returned

for the reward. Why, Jesse might have spent some of it."
She sobered and added, "If we don't act quick, he's likely
to have spent it all."

"He hasn't been in the area too long. That means he's
hidden the gold somewhere between Las Vegas and Raton
Pass, if he came that way. He might have come up from
Adobe Walls, but there's not much but prairie between here
and there. He'd not just bury it on the prairie or in the desert. He'd wanted something more solid to use as a hiding
place."

"Where he could do a map and have permanent landmarks."

Slocum looked at Audrey and wondered if she was being straight with him. So much gold had to be a powerful
lure. Was it stronger than the promise of seeing her name
on a front page story about Jesse James? Fame could trump
fortune, though Slocum thought fame was overrated.

"I might have an idea or two where he'd hole up. Men
like Jesse are predictable, if you've watched them long
enough."

"You'll help me!" Audrey squealed and threw her arms
around his neck and gave him a big wet kiss. Slocum wished
there was time for her to give him something more enjoy-
able to seal their deal, but he had to move fast to catch
Jesse. The outlaw had learned well from the likes of Quantrill and Anderson about constantly moving and never letting those pursing you to catch up.

"You go on into Las Vegas," he told her. "I can find
you there easier than anywhere else."

"Where are you going?"

Slocum wondered if the spring sun had given him heat
stroke or maybe the lure of gold jingling in his saddlebags
again was too powerful to deny. Hallucination or greed, it
didn't matter.

He was going to join up with Jesse and ride with the
James Gang.

4

Slocum edged back through the rocky crevice and came out
on the Las Vegas side, looking around for any hint that the
deputy had left lookouts. The entire posse must have ridden
off on the wild-goose chase that Audrey had set out for
them. That wouldn't last long. Either they would realize they
didn't have a trail to follow or the men would grow restive
and drift away. Only the promise of reward money kept most
of them on the trail. It was something of a poser for Slocum
that such a big posse had been mustered in such a short time.

Such was the power of Jesse James's name.

He rode back to where Jesse and the others had veered
away, leaving him the only quarry for the posse. The road
was too well traveled for him to decide which tracks be-
longed to Jesse and which were ordinary pilgrims along the
road. This broad road worked its way toward Raton Pass,
which saw a considerable amount of freight traffic. Bent's
Fort supplied not only Las Vegas but Taos and even Santa
Fe with goods brought in from back East.

Slocum drew rein when he saw a section of road that
looked different. His gut instinct worked for him now. He

rode a few yards off the road and found the tracks of a half-dozen horses. While this might have been a bunch of cowboys hunting for strays, he doubted it. The tracks were fresh and the horses had been galloping, as if their riders wanted to get out of sight of others along the road as quick as they could.

The tracks went back west into the foothills and rockier country. Then the trail split and each rider went in a different direction. Slocum frowned, spat some dust from his mouth, then picked one set of hoofprints to follow. Without knowing which was Jesse's horse, it didn't much matter who he followed. Frank James always seemed like an impulsive hothead, but Slocum didn't know him as well as he did his brother. The others were newcomers to the gang, but Slocum suspected they were all relatives of the James clan, even if the drop of blood binding them was scant.

Blood was thicker than water, and Slocum knew the James boys had spilled more than their share of both.

The tracks quickly disappeared as the rider traversed rocky ground. Slocum suspected that none of them was trying to hide where they rode now. They depended more on spreading the posse into segments rather than losing them all. Slocum snorted. He had been the one the posse had chosen. Sometimes Jesse was luckier than he was clever.

He watched the terrain around him closely, alert for any movement. If the gang had lit out thinking the law was on their tail, laying an ambush for anyone happening upon them wasn't much of a stretch. Slocum saw a broken branch on a small pine tree and rode for it. Someone had passed by recently since the sap still oozed from the wood. Slocum cocked his head to one side when he heard a horse neighing. He started to call out, then knew this was a sure way to get a bullet through the gut again. Jesse wanted him to ride along, but the others hadn't heard the invitation. To them he was only a stranger who'd happened to be in the saloon when the posse tried to round them up.

Slocum walked his horse into a rocky arena fifty feet in diameter. This would be a hell of a place to set up an ambush, but the man he followed wasn't on the rocks above. Slocum circled the pit and found the spot where the rider had stopped for a few minutes. Slocum frowned. It was as if the outlaw waited for something—or someone. If so, why had he ridden on? There hadn't been anyone else in the vicinity or Slocum would have heard them.

He dismounted and walked through the tumble of rocks until he came out on a cave. The outlaw he trailed was nowhere to be seen, but he had definitely stopped here also. Slocum saw where the man had tethered his horse for some time.

He listened hard. He was sure he had heard a horse neigh, but the steep rocks on all sides might have formed a funnel that brought distant sounds to his ear and made him think they were closer.

Cautiously approaching the mouth of the cave, Slocum strained every sense to catch a hint of what lay ahead. Blundering into a cave wasn't smart in the best of times because bears preferred them to more open, higher ground. He looked for bear spoor and saw nothing. Coyotes had been here frequently but nothing larger.

Slocum reached the mouth of the cave and looked into the depths. Only blackness ahead. He knew the outlaw wasn't here, but he entered the cave anyway. The inky dark surrounded him quickly. He started to strike a lucifer to get some idea where he was but hesitated. If anyone sat deeper in the cave, he would be a good target. When this thought hit him, he pressed himself against a cave wall to prevent the light from the mouth silhouetting him.

Inching ahead, he tried to find what had made this cave so interesting to one of the gang. In the darkness, he stepped down and the rock under his foot crumbled away. He threw himself backward, sat heavily, and still slid down into the unseen dark pit. Slocum flopped on his back and clutched wildly at the sides of the cave. His left hand found sharp rock. He winced as the stone cut his flesh, but he got a handhold that kept him from slipping farther. Then his grip began to give way as the blood turned his fingers slippery.

He flopped onto his belly and kicked hard with his boots, digging them into the sides of the pit. When he got enough purchase, he pushed hard, scooted along on his stomach, and reached firmer ground. Panting, he leaned against the wall and recovered his senses. The darkness didn't help him get his bearings, so he fumbled out the tin from his vest pocket and lit a lucifer. The sudden flare momentarily dazzled him, but before it burned to the end of the wood stick, he took in everything around him.

The pit yawned wide and deep to his right. The faint, flickering light wasn't strong enough to reveal the bottom. Slocum let out a low whistle realizing how lucky he had been. Then he let out another whistle as he looked up on the wall in front of him at the carefully lettered message.

He stood, dropped the match when it burned his fingers, then lit another to get a better gander at the wall. The symbols were interspersed with a series of four numbers, mostly ones and zeros. Now and then a larger number had been inserted, but the sequences were always four digits long.

Slocum had seen similar ciphers during the war. Each symbol relayed a word or phrase and the numbers gave more information, but about what he couldn't tell. He ran his finger over one number and it came away chalky. The message, whatever it meant, had been put here recently.

Slocum used one more match to examine the cave, but this time he did it on his knees so he could look at the dusty floor. Another set of fresh tracks were now obvious to him. His footprints went from side to side, but the others followed the wall with the message. Whoever had read the symbols knew the pit was only a step or two beyond and had stopped at the very edge of the message.

The pit hadn't been dug as a trap, but whoever had left the

message used what was already here to get rid of any snoops. Slocum took one last look at the message and then left the cave.

It wasn't hard to guess that the earlier visitor had been Jesse's henchman. Had he left the message or had he been sent here to read it? Slocum thought hard about the times he had seen similar codes during the war. Mostly, the guerrillas used them to show the way to friendly farmers or hidden caches of arms and supplies. Since Jesse came to New Mexico, he probably was only a step or two ahead of a federal marshal, and it made sense he would have supplies cached all over.

He had to laugh at the thought of Jesse James running away from a bounty hunter like Audrey. She was determined and smart, but she lacked the iron core necessary to pull the trigger and kill a man—and maybe even justify doing it with a shot to the back.

Slocum stepped outside and looked around. Something struck him as wrong. Then he heard it—or didn't hear it. There were no sounds of animals moving around, birds in the bushes, or . . . anything.

Reacting instinctively, he half twisted and dived behind a pile of rocks just as a bullet tore through the space where his head had been an instant before. He scrambled, got his feet under him, and had his six-shooter firmly in his grasp by the time he saw a flash of color. The sniper was atop a rock not thirty feet away when he carelessly exposed his arm. Slocum remembered the shirt pattern as belonging to one of the outlaws who had ridden with Frank on the train robbery. There hadn't been time to exchange introductions, so Slocum knew what he had to do.

Resting the butt of his Colt Navy against his left palm to steady his aim, he sighted in on the shirt sleeve still exposed. A single shot blasted forth, and the report was drowned out by the loud shriek of a man who'd just had his elbow blown off.

Slocum was ready for the next shot as the man reared up and grabbed for his wounded left arm. This round caught the man in the chest, sending him sliding down the far side of the boulder. The crash and grunt told him the man had hit the ground hard, but there was an additional sound that made him wary. The man was sobbing in pain.

That meant he was still dangerous.

Circling the boulder would have taken long minutes. Slocum had to get to the outlaw before he recovered. The elbow wound was probably the more serious, even if he had hit his target dead center in the man's chest. Slocum had seen men take twenty and thirty bullets during a raid and stay in the saddle, firing back at those who ventilated them. One had taken damned near a week to die.

Slocum didn't want any of the gang living that long to carry back the word to Jesse that Slocum had not only shot him up but had seen the message in the cave. Whatever the chalked message meant, it was important enough to put into code.

A fleeting thought came to Slocum. Audrey Underwood was less of a bounty hunter than she was a treasure hunter. She had the notion that the gang had brought plenty of gold with them. The message behind him might be a map of sorts to show the others where the loot had been buried.

Slocum got to the top of a small rock, holstered his six-gun, then jumped for all he was worth. His boots scraped repeatedly on the side of the boulder until he found purchase and began working his way upward like a four-legged spider. His hands were scraped raw when he got to the top where the sniper had lain in wait. A quick look confirmed what he already knew. A large pool of blood on the rock showed the damage he'd caused to the outlaw's elbow. A smaller drop of blood was all the evidence he had hit him with a second shot.

Drawing his six-shooter again, Slocum slid down the far side of the rock on the seat of his britches, landing hard

and stumbling forward. The outlaw had been doubly un-
lucky. When he had fallen off the boulder, he had crashed
down into a clump of Spanish bayonet. The sharp spines
jutting upward dripped gore, showing where the man had
impaled himself.

But there wasn't a body. He had pulled himself off the
foot-long rigid blades and stumbled away. Slocum went
after him.

As he rounded a bend, he found himself on the rim of a
deep ravine cut by spring runoff. The arroyo was dry, but
something new had been added. The outlaw lay sprawled
facedown on the sandy bottom. Slocum drew a bead on
him, but the man didn't stir. His back didn't move, and he
gave no sign of breathing. No blood pooled around him, but
Slocum wouldn't have expected that. The thirsty sand would
suck up any liquid dropped on it. More than this, dead men
didn't bleed.

He found a break in the steep rim and jumped down into
the arroyo, slipping and sliding. He recovered, his pistol
pointed at the man. Still no movement. He might be playing
possum. Slocum kicked him in the side and got no response.

Rolling him over told the real story. He hadn't landed
back down in the clump of Spanish bayonet. He had crashed
down so that his chest was impaled. Slocum saw a half-
dozen wounds, any of which might be mistaken for a knife
thrust. So much blood had soaked into the man's shirt,
Slocum couldn't even find his bullet wound. Stepping back,
he considered what he ought to do.

He had no way of finding Jesse James or any of the
others in the gang, but their dead partner might give him the
key to turn once he found the lock.

Slocum found the man's horse and brought it back. It
was messy, but he finally draped the limp body over the
saddle and then cinched it down so it wouldn't slide off. He

led the horse away, got his own, and rode back down the hillside until he came to a spot some distance from the cave. The man might have been going in that direction when misfortune felled him.

That was the story Slocum was going to tell if he found Jesse anytime soon.

He dropped the body from the saddle and tethered the horse where it could crop at some juicy grass. It would need watering before long, but if he was lucky, he would be back with the outlaw gang before it got too thirsty.

Slocum rode to the main road and joined a small wagon train, riding alongside as they rolled into Las Vegas. If the deputy or any of the other lawmen in the area were on the lookout for a solitary rider, he wouldn't make their hunt any easier.

As he rode down the main north-south street, he looked for a likely place where Audrey would have headed. A small café would do, even if the woman wasn't there. His belly growled and some food—and decent coffee—would go a ways toward restoring his good nature.

"John!"

He looked up and saw the woman in the doorway of the café, waving to him. His instincts about her had been right.

As he stepped up, Audrey's eyes went wide with shock. One hand covered her mouth and the other pointed at him.

"John, you're wounded!"

He looked down at the dried blood on his vest.

"Not mine," he said. She looked even more shocked at this. He took her by the arm and steered her back inside, out of sight of anyone in the street. Finding Jesse James might be hard, but he wanted to do it in his own way and at his own time.

"You ordered already?" He looked at where she had been sitting. A china cup of coffee sent tiny curls of steam into the air.

"I . . . yes. You want this?" She pushed the coffee toward him. He took a sip, then pushed it back. It wasn't any better than the coffee she had boiled over the campfire.

He pulled her down and sat across from her.

"I left one of the gang dead up in the hills," he said.

"Who? Which one?"

Slocum shrugged. He didn't know any of them save for the James brothers. As far as he was concerned, a dead outlaw was one less to hurrah a town or murder an innocent citizen. The time for such murdering ways was long past, and the James Gang didn't know it.

"There's something more important that I found in a cave." He looked at the tablecloth but knew drawing on it would mean taking it when he left. Any mark would be permanent on the bleached muslin.

He spread a napkin on the table, then asked, "You have a pencil?"

Audrey silently searched through her purse until she found a broken stub. He held it up and shook his head.

"What kind of reporter are you if this is the best you have? Never mind. Have you ever seen a code like this before?" He quickly sketched out the symbols but omitted the numbers.

"I think so. At least I've heard about caves where people found such things. They claimed they were put there by the Freemasons to mark their territory, but they don't look like any Freemason symbols I've ever seen."

Although it was possible that Jesse James was a Freemason, Slocum doubted it. Prone to secrecy, yes. The outlaw was suited for that. But Slocum could never imagine him taking part in what was supposed to be elaborate rituals while dressed in crazy, colorful robes.

"Do you know anyone who might decipher them?"

"How can I send these over a telegraph? My editor might recognize them. Mr. Herschel knows a little bit about everything, or at least it seems that way. But it would take far too long to send a copy by mail to him and even longer to get a response."

Slocum had already come to that conclusion. He had hoped Audrey, in her tracking down of the James Gang, had seen something similar before.

"Was there anything more to the message?" Audrey asked. "This looks so . . . incomplete."

"You think it might be a map of some kind?"

"To where they hid gold?" The woman's eyes went wide as the idea of a fortune buried up in the mountains made her news story seem less important. Greed always did that, at least in Slocum's experience, but as eager as she might be to find the gold, too many barriers stood in the way.

Not the least of which was being unable to decipher the code.

Slocum leaned back in the chair as he thought on the biggest obstacle in the way of being filthy rich.

Jesse James wasn't the sort to give up stolen gold graciously. He would gun down his own brother if Frank thought to steal from him.

What he would do to anyone else wasn't comfortable to think on.

"I have to join the gang," Slocum said. "It's the only way."

Audrey Underwood stared at him. He wasn't sure he liked the tiny smile curling her perfect lips and what it might mean.

5

"I want to see the spot where you found this cipher," Audrey Underwood said. "I can be working on its meaning while you find Jesse James and enlist."

"It's not like he is recruiting an army unit," Slocum said. It irritated him thinking of Jesse and the C.S.A. There had been nothing military about the way the guerrilla bands had fought or killed.

"Do you think the Fort Union soldiers will come after him if they get wind of him being in the territory?"

Slocum had considered this and doubted it would happen. The cavalry had more to do than go on wild chases across the countryside trying to find a will-'o-the-wisp like Jesse James. He had outmaneuvered regular Federal soldiers for too long not to know their ways. Fort Union was a supply depot and responsible for maintaining a string of forts throughout the region. Slocum told Audrey this.

"That's something of a relief," she said. "Less competition for me to bring him in."

"You're back to pretending to be a bounty hunter?"

"I am," she said, irritated. "I'm also a reporter. When

one job is impossible, I shall pursue the other to the utmost. That way, I'm never out of work."

"Stick to reporting. The *Las Vegas Optic* might need a reporter."

"I've inquired. The editor was quite rude to me, saying they didn't believe a woman could report the news. They probably thought I couldn't even write. Why, they refused to even look at clippings of my other stories already published."

"Fancy that," Slocum said dryly. He cared less about Audrey finding a job than he did about her getting gunned down pretending to be a bounty hunter. Jesse didn't have much of a sense of humor when it came to getting arrested and locked up for the rest of his life in prison—or getting his neck stretched by a hangman's noose.

"Will you take me to the spot where you found the coded message?"

Slocum hesitated and didn't know why. There couldn't be any harm in Audrey studying the cipher to see what she could make of it. Although he had seen similar markings during the war, he might have missed something important. A key might have been scratched into the rock away from the message, a key that would reveal the meaning of the message. It might be nothing more than telling Jesse's gang where to meet after a robbery or it could be significant.

Gold. The golden lure still poked him in the gut. Jesse James had stolen a fair amount in his day and none of it had ever been recovered. Most folks thought Jesse gave it to the poor, but Slocum knew Jesse James would keep it for himself. Hiding it in New Mexico might be smart since it was far away from the scene of so many of his successful robberies. Jesse could come to Las Vegas and retire, secure because of a cave loaded with gold he had stolen back in Missouri and Kansas.

"It's too dangerous right now. My ticket into the gang is stashed not far from the cave. If Jesse even gets a hint that somebody knows where his message rock is, he'll move everything."

"That's true," Audrey said, looking thoughtful. "He is a cautious man when it comes to hiding his gold. I've figured that out already from my study of his character."

"You stay in town and let me find him. When it's safe—and when I know he's not going to change the message—I'll let you know."

"I'm staying at a boardinghouse just on the edge of town. Senora Gonzalez said I could rent the room by the week or month. I've taken it only for a week."

"I'll find the place," Slocum assured her.

They sat staring at one another across the table for a long minute. Slocum couldn't guess what ran through Audrey's mind, but it wasn't what occupied his. She was as much after the James Gang gold as he was, but she had other chances to make her own fortune. A detailed story about the capture and hanging of Jesse James would bring her both notoriety and a modicum of money. She didn't have a snowball's chance in hell of actually capturing Jesse and turning him in for the reward. Where she had gotten the crazy notion she could be a bounty hunter simply by declaring herself to be one made Slocum wonder if she'd been hit on the head recently. Or maybe she had just never come up against a cold-blooded killer like Jesse James and had no idea how difficult arresting him would be.

"I need to ride," Slocum said. He stood. She reached out impulsively and gripped his arm.

"John, be careful. You shouldn't needlessly risk your neck for me."

He kept from laughing. She thought he did this to further her career? He did it for the gold.

"I'm always careful," he said.

"You weren't so careful up there above the gap after the posse left."

Slocum wasn't going to argue that point. But Audrey

thought she had bound him to her with a brief fling. She had quite an opinion of herself and her abilities.

He left the café and went to the saloon, looking inside to see if Jesse might have returned. The outlaw was a bold one, arrogant and willing to flout authority. It would be something he did, coming to town to drink while the posse scoured the hills hunting for him.

Although it might be something he would do, the outlaw had chosen not to drink here and now. Slocum got his horse and rode from town toward the spot where the gang had left the road before. The one trail led to the cave where Slocum had found the message scribbled on the wall—and not far from there was the dead body of a gang member. Slocum intended to use that corpse as his way into the gang.

If he could find Jesse James.

Taking a different trail proved more productive for him. Only an hour's ride brought him into the foothills again where he spied a tiny spiral of smoke. He took a deep whiff. Somebody cooked a late afternoon meal of venison. It never paid to just ride up unannounced, so he approached slowly and was immediately glad that he did.

Frank James stood on a rock to his right, rifle pulled in tight to his shoulder.

"No closer," the outlaw shouted.

"It's me, Slocum. I want to talk to your brother. I got some bad news for him."

Frank lowered the rifle and got a better look. He motioned with the rifle barrel that Slocum was to advance. Then he disappeared down the far side of the rock. By the time Slocum had ridden the twenty yards to the base of the large rock, Frank James had come around to peer up at him.

"Not sure Jesse wants to talk with you, Slocum. He's in a mean mood right about now."

"It'll get worse."

"Hell, come on through. We can use a bit of excitement if he decides to use you for target practice."

Slocum rode along the winding path through the rocks, aware that Frank followed with the rifle aimed at his exposed back. He came to a halt a few yards away from the campfire and waited for Jesse to notice him. He was sure the outlaw had been aware of his approach from the instant his brother had called out the challenge.

Jesse finally dropped the piece of meat he was eating into the fire where it sizzled and popped, sending hot fat spattering in all directions. Two of the gang nearby turned from it rather than have the boiling fat hit their faces. Jesse was oblivious.

"He said he's got bad news, Jesse," Frank called. "You want him to get some bad news, too?"

Slocum knew that a single word from his brother would give Frank permission to shoot him in the back.

"What is it, Slocum?"

"I found one of your gang dead. And I don't think he was killed by the posse."

"Who was it?"

Slocum described him the best he could, finishing with, "He had a half-dozen knife wounds in the chest. I left him a few miles up into the hills."

"Why didn't you bury him?"

"I wasn't getting paid for it," Slocum said.

Jesse scowled at him, then burst out laughing. He motioned for Slocum to step down and sit at the fire.

"I forgot what a joker you are, Slocum. You got a real sense of humor. Hell, I wouldn't have buried him, either, and he rode with us for damned near a month."

"Who was he?"

"Names don't make no nevermind to the dead. If you want to collect the bounty on his head, take him into Las Vegas and let the marshal find a wanted poster." Jesse looked hard at Slocum. "You won't do that 'cuz there's like to be a poster on you. Isn't that so?"

"Can't dispute it," Slocum said. There was one still making its way throughout the West for judge killing. After Bill Anderson had gut shot him, Slocum had taken a long time to recuperate and had finally returned to Slocum's Stand in Calhoun, Georgia, to settle down. All he wanted to do was grow crops on the family farm he had inherited, but a carpetbagger judge had taken a fancy to the land and had come to seize it for unpaid taxes. He and a hired gunman had ridden out to proclaim the foreclosure and only one had ridden away from the farm—John Slocum. He had buried the bodies by the springhouse and had never looked back.

The law against killing a federal judge, carpetbagger deserving it or not, was one that marshals throughout the country enforced. It had been a spell since Slocum had seen a poster offering a hundred-dollar reward for his capture for that crime. But he didn't doubt that a few yellowed, brittle copies of the wanted poster with his likeness were still in files in marshals' offices where he least expected.

"Why are you talkin' to him, Jesse? Put a bullet in him and let's get outta here," Charlie Dennison said.

"Keep fingering your pistol like that and you won't be doing any moving except six feet under," Slocum said.

Dennison half stood, hand flashing to his six-shooter. He froze when he found himself staring down the barrel of Slocum's Colt.

"Go on, shoot him," Jesse said.

Slocum wasn't sure who the outlaw was speaking to.

"Sit down," he ordered Dennison. "Or you can fall over with a bullet in your head."

Dennison's hand shook, as if he restrained himself from drawing. Then he relaxed and settled back to the rock on the other side of the fire. Slocum knew he had made himself an enemy, but then Charlie Dennison hadn't been much of a friend before. From what Slocum had heard about him, Dennison would rob a widow of her egg money.

A collective sigh passed through the others who had watched. Slocum knew they were disappointed blood hadn't been spilled. Most likely, they didn't like Dennison any more than he did but would have cheered Dennison on if he had killed the interloper. About the only entertainment men like this got was seeing somebody die.

"Now that the two dogs have got done snarling at each other," Jesse said, "I asked you before if you wanted to join up, Slocum. If what you say is true, I'm a man shy."

"Don't do this, Jesse," Frank said. "I don't like his looks. Remember what Bloody Bill—"

"Quiet, Frank. Slocum is a straight shooter. If he gives his word, that's enough for me. He might have had a moment's break in his faith, but he rode with Bill Quantrill, same as us. That has to count for something. Isn't that right, Slocum?"

"It means something to me," Slocum said.

"See, Frank? Slocum is all right. Now what do you think happened to the, uh, gent you found?"

"Can't say. The way he was all cut up, looked like he tangled with an Indian and lost."

"There's no Indians around right now," Dennison said sullenly. "We got this whole damned place to ourselves."

"Charlie has a point," Jesse said. "Those boys in blue over at Fort Union have run off the Navajo, and the Comanche are kicking up their heels down south a ways from here. Them Injuns from the pueblos don't count, and this is a bit far north for the Apache to come raiding. We'd have heard if a band of them was in the region."

"There are hunters in the Sangre de Cristos. Might be he crossed one of them."

"Might be Slocum killed him thinking to join up to replace him," Dennison said. "Might be Slocum put a couple rounds in him."

"That's true. What red-blooded son of the South wouldn't do what it took to join us in our noble endeavor?" Jesse asked. The men all nodded agreement. Slocum tensed. This didn't sound like the James Gang had come to New Mexico to hide out, nor did it sound as if they intended to rob their way through the territory. Something else was in the wind.

Slocum felt the hair on the back of his neck rise and knew Frank James had the rifle trained on him. He was dedicated to his brother but might go along with Charlie Dennison if Jesse showed the slightest hesitation.

Slocum breathed a tad easier when Jesse said, "John, why don't we all mosey on over to where you found our late, lamented friend so we can see the truth of your statements."

"You calling me a liar, Jesse?" Slocum knew better than to call out the outlaw, but he also knew that Jesse would expect him to be bristly over having his story questioned.

"Not yet, John, not yet. Mount up, boys. We're going for an afternoon ride."

Slocum kept telling himself he stood to find a mountain of gold, but getting there was going to mean enduring a considerable risk. This wasn't new for him, but it didn't make him ride any easier knowing Frank had an itchy trigger finger and Charlie Dennison just wanted to kill him for the pleasure of seeing him die.

"Up there," Slocum said, recognizing the spot where he had left the body. He forced himself to keep from looking higher on the hillside, along the trail toward the cave with the chalk code marked on the wall. If one of Jesse's gang had been up there, it probably meant the others knew about it. From the way they were getting edgier as they rode, he knew he was right.

"Yup, he's dead, Jesse," Frank said, kicking the dead man's ribs. "And Slocum was right about him getting stabbed to death." Frank James pulled back the shirt, peeling the cloth away from the dried blood. He probed and finally said, "Looks like he was done in with a small knife. Never seen anything like this before, but then I don't bother with that many bodies." Frank stood and laughed. "Mostly I just shoot 'em and leave 'em where they fall."

This produced laughter from the others in the gang. Slocum was more intent on Jesse's reaction. The two of them ended up staring at each other. The outlaw's pale eyes bored into him, and Slocum didn't flinch.

"You been any farther along this trail, Slocum?"

"I came from that direction," Slocum said, pointing to the south. "I never heard a thing, but I saw his horse."

"Charlie, you take the horse. We can always use another," Jesse called. To Slocum he said, "Let's you and me take a ride. Up the trail."

Slocum rode behind the outlaw, wondering what was going to happen. The winding trail cut them off from the others, who remained behind. The farther west they rode, the closer they got to the cave. When it became apparent Jesse was riding straight for the cave, Slocum began worrying that he had left evidence of being inside.

"Dismount, Slocum. I got something to show you."

Jesse went into the cave ahead of him. Slocum knew how dark it was there and entered warily. As Slocum had guessed the other outlaw had done, Jesse followed the left wall, pressing close and advancing cautiously. Slocum dared not reveal he knew anything about their destination—or the deep pit.

"You got a light, Slocum? It's mighty dark in here."

"Got a lucifer," Slocum said. He went cold inside when he saw Jesse standing a few feet ahead, his boot next to the stub of a match Slocum had dropped earlier. Slocum hastily lit the match and held it up high. The faint light didn't reveal the pit. He walked forward until he stood on the burnt match on the ground. Trying to remember how many matches he had lit before and where they might be made sweat break out on his forehead.

"Come a bit closer. To your left," Jesse said. "You don't want to get too far into this cave since there's one hell of a fall if you find the shaft a couple feet farther."

Slocum relaxed a little. If Jesse had intended to kill him,

that would have been the easiest way since he wouldn't have had to waste a bullet.

"What's that?" Slocum asked, pointing to the cipher on the cave wall.

"I wanted you to see this. You recognize it?"

"I saw code like this during the war, but I don't recognize any of these symbols," Slocum said.

"Of course not. This is a brand spanking new code."

"What's it say?"

"I got something to ask you, Slocum. You happy with the way the war ended?"

"Too many good men died. Can't be happy about that."

"The South died, dammit! The carpetbaggers flocked down and stole everything that wasn't blown up or burned down during the war, leaving us nothing. Nothing!" Jesse James was getting worked up now, waving his arms around. His voice rose and turned shriller as emotion took control.

Slocum said nothing. He had wanted to find what the code meant, and Jesse was fixing to tell him.

"Some of us aren't going to sit back and do nothing. Before the war, you heard of the Knights of the Golden Circle. They changed and became as weak as tea. But some of them—some of us—aren't going to let that situation go on any longer."

Slocum wasn't exactly sure what Jesse was saying, but he didn't like the sound of it.

"Me and the boys have come to New Mexico for a reason, Slocum. I want you to join us."

"Join you to do what?" Slocum knew what the outlaw was going to say but he had to ask anyway.

"Throw in with us and the rest of the Knights of the Golden Circle so we can take over the whole damned territory and make our own country."

6

"You have to realize that this isn't a pipe dream, Slocum," Jesse James went on, his eyes wide as he became more animated. He had a weak eye and it began to roam as his agitation grew. "We can do this. We've cached the gold to finance the whole damned operation."

"What are you going to do?"

"This," Jesse said, tapping the chalk markings on the wall. "This is part of our scheme. We can make this happen, Slocum. We can!"

"What are you intending to do? You can't take on the entire New Mexico Territory."

"But we can. We're not alone. There are several powerful men backing us up. The Knights of the Golden Circle will be complete. We'll turn the Southwest into a new country and merge with Mexico and the countries in Central America."

"I heard tell you'd get the Caribbean islands involved, too, but that was before the war."

"This is now, Slocum. We're going to do it *now*. We'll forge the Golden Circle. The Caribbean, Central America, the Southwest. We'll be a country united in our belief that slavery is right."

"We fought over that and lost," Slocum said.

"We were sold out. Oh, not the generals but the politicians. They were paid off. Do you believe that Jeff Davis did all he could to win? He was a weak president. We should have had someone stronger to hold the reins of power. Why have the capital in Richmond when it should have been in the Deep South? Georgia or Alabama. He did everything wrong and might have been paid to lose the war for us."

"Davis didn't lose the war. We did."

"We won't this time. We'll be stronger than ever. When the Golden Circle is a fact, we can move back into Florida and up the coast. We can strangle the damned Yankees and take back what's rightfully ours."

"You say you have the gold to do this?"

"Oh, yes, Slocum, we do. I've got it cached for when it'll do us the most good."

"You need more than money," Slocum said. "You need to stop the Federals at Fort Union. There's a powerful lot of them that won't cotton much to you taking over the territory."

"Don't worry about them. We'll have our army when the time is right—and it's getting real close, Slocum. Real close."

Slocum heard more than avarice and ambition in Jesse James's voice. He heard a hint of the madness that had infected Quantrill and Anderson and so many others in the guerrilla band. Hindsight told him they had been fighting a losing war but had never believed that because of the infectious words of men like Quantrill. Facts meant nothing and faith was everything.

That worked. For a while. Eventually reality intruded and their illusions had to crash to the ground like a shattered looking glass. Slocum could hear the same deadly sound in Jesse's words.

"You been working on this for a while?"

"It's all figured out," he said. "When the time is right, we'll use the gold to bribe the right people."

"Politicians who can be bought won't stay bought," Slocum said.

"You're right. That's why I'm not bribing politicians," Jesse said. "The Knights of the Golden Circle will be in control of the entire northern part of New Mexico within a month. We'll control the roads and cut off Taos and Santa Fe from their supplies unless they side with us. And they will. Why shouldn't they? The people have been under the Yankee thumb long enough to know we offer them freedom."

"And slavery," Slocum said.

"What else would you do with all those redskins? They're killers and don't deserve to be free. We can make them work and bring riches to the whole territory."

"Killers," Slocum said, almost under his breath. He knew who the killers were and he was in a cave with one.

"Damned right! We'll be rulers over an entire country. Think about that, Slocum. How'd you like to run an entire state? You're a smart fellow. When we take Santa Fe, you can be governor."

"You fixing to be president?"

"Why not? The Knights of the Golden Circle need a strong leader. You can't deny that I've held my family together. The whole damned territory will be a new family for me, a bigger one."

"So what's the purpose of the code?" Slocum asked.

"We need a way of communicating with the others so we don't have to meet in public. If the marshal saw us all together, he'd get suspicious. And the people in Las Vegas don't know how good they'll have it when the Knights pick up the reins of power."

"What's this tell us?"

Jesse began explaining the code, working from one side to the other. He finished at the numbers.

"There's a shipment of rifles and ammunition to the fort due anytime now. This is tomorrow's date. The other part of the code tells the road where the shipment's being sent."

"And this?" Slocum pointed to another section of the code. "Does this tell how many guards'll be with the wagon train?"

"I was right about you, Slocum. It does," Jesse muttered to himself, counting on his fingers as he deciphered the code, then said, "Ten men will guard the wagons. Three wagons, ten guards, plus the drivers."

"That'll be quite a fight. You don't have that many men, and the Army will be expecting an attack."

"No, they won't. That's what makes the plan so perfect. We get the guns, and we'll be ready for the final phase of the revolt."

"You'll need an army," Slocum said, trying to get something more out of the outlaw.

"I got it all worked out, Slocum. It's all up here." He tapped his head. "Now we got to move. This here message tells us all we have to know." He stopped and peered at the chalk marks in the faint light. "A pity he went and got himself killed. It's going to be quite a ride getting to the ambush. But we're used to that, aren't we?" Jesse slapped Slocum on the back and strutted off, whistling "Goober Peas."

Slocum trailed him, considering that Jesse must trust him or he wouldn't have turned his back on him. Or did the outlaw simply know Slocum well enough that back shooting wasn't in his nature?

"We got to ride hard. Mount up, Slocum. We're on the road to destiny!"

With a loud rebel yell, Jesse James galloped off. If Slocum had a lick of sense, he would have fallen behind and then slipped away, heading south as hard as he could ride. He'd been in Santa Fe and had no desire to see the dusty, sleepy town again but that quiet would go a ways toward soothing his nerves after listening to Jesse's cockeyed scheme to seize control of the entire territory and turn it into a new slave-holding country.

Or was it so cockeyed? Slocum had the sinking feeling that, with enough gold for bribes, the politicians and businessmen in the territory might go along with Jesse. There had to be some resentment festering among those who paid taxes to Washington and got damned little back for it. Other than the cavalry and their string of forts, the excise taxes gave the citizens nothing back. It was the same throughout the South. The Northerners moved in with the force of the law behind them and taxed and virtually enslaved the population.

Slocum could have gotten away, but the lure of the gold required to buy an entire country spurred him on. Audrey had mentioned the sum of ten thousand dollars. It would take that—and more. He followed Jesse back to where the others still stood around the moldering body. They hadn't bothered to bury their partner.

"I got the information we need. We ride north, men," Jesse said. "And keep your guns at hand. The wagons'll be guarded by ten soldiers."

"That all?" Dennison scoffed and looked around. "Hell, Jesse, you can take 'em all by your lonesome."

"You don't want to miss the fun, Charlie," Frank James said. "We're gonna be kings 'fore you know it."

Slocum wondered what Jesse had promised his gang. The sun and moon and stars above, from the sound of it, were all going to be theirs after the revolt. Men like Dennison would be content with killing, but the others needed more of a reward.

"Fifteen miles north of Las Vegas," Jesse said. "That's where the wagon train will come across from the east before picking up the road down to Fort Union."

"We're with you, Jesse. All the way!"

Slocum wasn't sure who picked up the cheer, but he

found himself going along with it. He was glad he did because as the last hurrah died on his lips, he saw Jesse staring right at him. The outlaw leader smiled, tipped his hat in Slocum's direction, and then put his heels to his horse's flanks.

"I see the wagons!" Frank James shouted from the top of a scrubby cottonwood. He waved so frantically to signal the approach that he nearly fell out amid wildly shaking leaves and spindly limbs. He caught himself, then shinnied down the trunk to land on the ground next to his brother. "It's just like you said, Jesse. Three wagons, the drivers, and ten guards. The way they're riding, they don't expect a hint of trouble to come their way."

"Well, they're right," Jesse said. "They're not going to get a hint of trouble. They're going to get a shitload of it!"

The gang cheered. This time Slocum remained silent, trying to judge what he ought to do. The gang didn't bother with bandannas over their faces. Slocum knew that meant no one in the wagon train was going to walk away from the robbery. He had been on more than one raid during the war where it was assumed that this meant death to everyone setting eyes on them.

"Mount up. You know what to do," Jesse said. He looked at Slocum, eyes hard. "Ride with me." He turned his horse's face and galloped off in the direction of the wagons. Slocum followed. He had little choice but to go along with the massacre because Jesse and the others would hunt him down since he knew too much of their plans now.

Slocum scoffed at the notion of an independent state being carved out of New Mexico Territory, but Jesse James wasn't joking. If he had the gold, he was now going for the weapons to bring about his dream of a country allied with the Knights of the Golden Circle.

All that Jesse lacked were the soldiers to ride under his banner. From the way he had spoken so confidently, that wasn't going to be a problem either. Slocum had no choice. He galloped after the outlaw in time to hear the first ragged volley of shots from the wagon train's guards.

He burst through a cloud of dust and saw that the gang's initial attack hadn't been coordinated. One half had jumped the gun and alerted the soldiers so that they jumped into the wagons and fired from the relative safety of the wagon beds.

"They've got all the ammo they need to hold us off," Slocum shouted. "Pull back and regroup."

The gang closest to him reacted to the sharp edge of command in his voice. Those on the far side couldn't hear his orders because of the increasing reports from the soldiers' return fire nor could they see because of the billowing cloud of white gun smoke rising.

"What do we do?" asked a youngster. He looked panicked.

"This your first raid?" Slocum asked. He got a quick nod in reply. "Stay behind me and make sure none of the soldiers sneaks off. We don't want them getting reinforcements." Slocum doubted this would happen, but it kept the anxious outlaw from shooting him in the back.

Slocum put his head down and raced forward. Bullets sang past him and the acrid stench of gunpowder made his nostrils flare. He pulled parallel with the wagon as a soldier reared up to fire. Reaching out, Slocum snared the rifle barrel and tugged hard, sending the bluecoat tumbling to the ground.

Galloping on, Slocum drew his six-shooter and fired twice at the soldier crouching in the rear of the wagon. The soldier never saw him, being intent on Charlie Dennison charging at him from the other side. The soldier gasped and slumped in the wagon bed. Slocum had winged him, but from the way he gasped and spit blood, he might not live long.

"Damn you, Slocum. He was mine!" Dennison roared.

He turned his rifle on two soldiers crouched under the second wagon.

And then the silence descending on the battlefield clutched at Slocum's heart. No more firing meant the soldiers and drivers were dead. It took Jesse James a few seconds to realize he had triumphed. He led his men in a rousing victory cheer.

Slocum rode back to the wagon and looked down at the soldier he had pulled from the wagon. He stirred and sat up, groggy from the fall. Slocum jumped from the saddle and knelt beside the man, whispering, "If you want to live, fake being dead." He fired his six-gun so the slug ripped away part of the man's scalp. Such wounds bled like a son of a bitch and the shock knocked the soldier out.

"Good work, Slocum," Jesse said, thinking Slocum had performed the coup de grâce. "I'm glad I wasn't wrong dealing you into this game."

"It's not a game," Slocum said, standing so he blocked the soldier from Jesse's direct view. The shallow breathing would be a giveaway—a dead giveaway from both the soldier and Slocum.

"No, you're right. The Knights of the Golden Circle is deadly serious. To independence!"

Jesse's shout was picked up by the others.

While they celebrated by riding in circles around the wagons and the bodies of their victims, Slocum looked into the back of the wagon at the man he had shot. As careful as he had been, the man had died from his wound. Slocum pulled him out and then saw he wasn't exactly right. Three other bullet wounds in the man's chest had added to the chances of the man dying. Slocum's final bullet might have pushed him over the edge, but if anything, he had given the man a more merciful death. The other wounds were fatal—slowly fatal.

He yanked back the canvas and saw crates of cavalry

carbines. Making a quick inventory told him Jesse had just acquired more than a hundred rifles in this single wagon.

"We got ammunition in this one," Frank James called. "We got it all, Jesse. We got it all and didn't lose a single man!"

A new cheer went up, but Slocum turned wary. It hadn't been an easy victory, but it had been too easy.

"Jesse," he called. "Jesse! We got to get out of here fast. Something's wrong."

"Nothing's wrong," Jesse James said. "We just won our first battle for independence. There's—"

A distant bugle signaled the arrival of a larger cavalry troop.

"Frank, we got company coming. Maybe an entire company!" Jesse laughed, a note of insanity in his voice. "You and Charlie get the wagons out of here. Hide the cargo while the rest of us lead the bluecoats on a wild-goose chase."

Slocum dragged the soldier he had knocked out from under the wheels to prevent him from getting run over as Frank James snapped the reins and got the load of rifles rattling forward. The soldier's eyelids fluttered and he looked up, finally focusing on Slocum's face.

"Stay quiet. There's a company from Fort Union coming this way," Slocum said. He swung into the saddle, shot the soldier in the dust a dark look to keep him from trying to be a hero by drawing his pistol and blazing away at the outlaws. Then he rode off. He had done what he could for the soldier. It was up to him to decide if he wanted a posthumous medal or preferred a chance to eat rotten food in the fort mess hall again.

"Where are they heading?" Slocum called to Jesse. He pointed to Frank and Charlie driving at breakneck speed back along the road.

"Don't ask. We got to decoy them bluecoats away so they have a chance."

"How?"

"The survivors will come after us if we kill enough of them. That or the ones not filled with good Southern lead will turn tail and run whining back to their fort."

Jesse laughed as he wheeled about and brought the rifle to his shoulder. He began firing when the lead element of the horse soldiers thundered into view. They raced past the point of the ambush and came on.

Slocum saw that he had no other choice. The soldiers would run him to the ground if they didn't break off their attack. He pulled his Winchester and fired low, bullets skipping across the ground and nicking horses' legs. This created more confusion among the attacking soldiers than if he had felled one or two of them.

Jesse motioned and rode due east. The wagons had driven north. The officer in command shouted at his men to regroup. A half dozen were left on foot because of the wounds Slocum had inflicted on their horses. He hoped that they'd find the soldier he had saved since the man required some first aid but wasn't in any danger of dying.

Why he cared was beyond him—he had spent the war killing men wearing Federal uniforms. Then he realized why he had gone to such lengths and risked his own life. The war was over, and he didn't want Jesse James or anyone else reigniting it. He had fled West to get away from the outcome of the war and had found riding the range a freedom denied him before. Jesse threatened that freedom if he plunged New Mexico into a war he could never win. Before it had been North against South. This time it would be North and South against New Mexico. Those odds were even worse than the ones Robert E. Lee had faced.

And Lee had surrendered at Appomattox. Slocum doubted Jesse James would ever have sense enough to pass over his sword.

"Keep riding," Slocum shouted to the youngster he had befriended during the attack.

"Can't. Horse is pulling up lame."

Slocum rode closer, matched speed, and then said, "Get behind me. My mare's strong enough for both our weights."

The man jumped, slipped, and clung to Slocum's saddlebags long enough to regain his balance and pull himself up on the horse's hindquarters.

Slocum felt his horse begin to weaken right away, but she kept running. Jesse and the rest of the gang had disappeared into a bosque ahead. If he followed, he would get lost and become easy pickings for the pursuing bluecoats.

Slocum veered away and rode for a hilly section. If he could stay out of the direct line of sight, he had a chance of losing the soldiers hot on his trail.

At least, he hoped he could. With the weight doubled on his horse, he could never outrun the troopers.

"Mind if I say a prayer?" the man behind him asked.

"Say one for me, too. We're going to need all the help we can get."

Slocum turned abruptly and guided his horse into a shallow arroyo. He heard the bugle blaring commands for the cavalry to come after him as his horse faltered and then came to a halt, unable to push on.

"Get ready to fight," Slocum said, dropping to the ground and pulling his six-shooter. He turned and waited for the fight of his life to begin.

7

"We're gonna die, aren't we?" The young outlaw stared at Slocum without much emotion. "And I never got a chance to do much."

"We're not dead yet," Slocum said. He checked his six-shooter and tried to ignore the sound of the approaching bugle blaring out its commands to the company of horse soldiers intent on shooting them down like dogs. Slocum had been in tight spots before and gotten out by thinking and not panicking.

"They'll find my horse and know one of us is on foot," the outlaw said.

"They will," Slocum said as a plan formed. "They'll expect us to get as far away as possible, not to attack them, except from ambush."

"So we ambush them? I don't have much ammunition."

"Won't need it," Slocum said. "Come on. Stay low." He estimated where the outlaw's horse would be found and knew what the commanding officer's reaction would be to it.

He left his horse behind and ran down the arroyo, using the bank as cover until he got a hundred yards back in the direction he had ridden. Slocum chanced a quick look over the bank and saw a sergeant ordering four soldiers to fan out and hunt for the outlaw on foot. Then the sergeant ordered the rest of his squad to continue along the trail, heading in the direction Slocum had hoped. The noncom rode away along a trail Slocum would have followed if he hadn't been burdened with a second rider on his horse.

"What do we do? Shoot them?" The young outlaw had his six-gun out. His hand shook slightly.

"You ever kill anybody before?"

"No."

"Don't start now. No shooting." Slocum put his finger against his lips when he heard the crunch of boots on the ground above his head. A soldier came to the arroyo to see if the rider from the lame horse had come this way.

Slocum holstered his six-shooter and reached up, grabbed a handful of wool uniform, and pulled hard. The soldier let out a yelp of surprise and crashed to the ground at Slocum's feet. Before the bluecoat could regain his senses, the outlaw with Slocum clubbed their victim.

Slocum nodded once to his partner, then pressed back against the sandy embankment and let out a low moan and mumbled, "Help me, dammit. I fell!"

A second soldier peered over and saw only his comrade on the ground. Slocum grabbed, missed, and started to recover but found himself with an armful of struggling, shouting soldier when the outlaw grappled with him. The three of them went down in a pile on the sandy bottom of the arroyo. Between them, Slocum and the outlaw muffled the soldier's outcry. It took only a few seconds to club him unconscious, too.

Pointing down the riverbed, Slocum silently sent his partner a few yards away. He knew the outlaw couldn't move silently—and didn't. He drew the attention of the third soldier.

"Hands up!" The soldier leveled his carbine. The trap

would have worked better if the outlaw hadn't looked at Slocum.

Swarming up the side of the arroyo, Slocum tackled the soldier and sent him tumbling down where the outlaw made quick work of him.

"You, hands up!" The fourth soldier had come running up at the disturbance.

Slocum slowly stood, standing at the rim of the arroyo. He didn't make the mistake of looking at the outlaw, who clutched his pistol and looked determined. And why not? They had taken out three bluecoats without firing a shot.

"You got it wrong, Corporal," Slocum said. He kept his hands high and began to circle. "That's not my horse over there. Mine's down in the arroyo. I heard a ruckus and came to see what was going on when a soldier went flopping over the edge. He's down there now hurt bad."

"Don't try anything," the soldier said. He looked suspiciously at Slocum and gripped the rifle hard. Hardly older than the outlaw hiding in the arroyo, the soldier edged to the arroyo. As he came close to the edge, Slocum lowered his hands and turned fast. The soldier reacted as Slocum had thought, giving him his entire attention.

The outlaw grabbed the soldier's ankles and yanked hard, sending him crashing face first to the ground. Slocum was already moving and slugged the soldier before he could recover.

"We did it, Slocum. We got all four of them."

"Tie 'em up," Slocum said.

"We can kill them."

"No need, unless you want to shoot four unconscious men. You up for that?"

"Don't reckon I am," the youngster said. "What'd Jesse do?"

"That shouldn't matter. What do you do?" Slocum ripped away part of the soldier's jacket into a strip and bound his hands behind his back, then gagged him.

"My name's Zeke."

"Get to work, Zeke. Take their weapons, and I'll fetch their horses."

This touch of theft appealed to the outlaw. By the time Slocum had brought the four troopers' horses to the arroyo, Zeke had finished binding their prisoners.

"Horse thievin'. That's something Jesse would approve of."

"Always has," Slocum said, handing over the reins to his partner. "I'll fetch my horse. Get your gear from yours. Don't leave behind anything that'll make it easier for them to identify us."

"They couldn't if we killed them."

"Save your ammo for when it matters," Slocum said. He knew Jesse James affected those in his gang. The ones that weren't family were friends of his family. Where Zeke fit in wasn't something he wanted to know. For a scheme as grand as Jesse was spinning, he'd recruit anyone wanting to ride with him. It would take a lot of guns to seize control of an entire U.S. territory and establish a new slave country.

It would take a lot of rebels.

"You been riding with Jesse for long, Slocum?"

"Not so long, but I knew him during the war."

"That must have been great." Zeke waited for Slocum to regale him with war stories, but Slocum wasn't inclined. He had no good memories, and the young man had been sucked into a whirlpool so strong he wasn't likely to win free, no matter what Slocum said. Anything good about Jesse James would only cement Zeke's desire to be a part of a crazy revolutionary scheme. And he would never believe the truth about the outlaw.

"We need to cut toward the mountains," Slocum said, reading the trail left by the sergeant's detachment. The soldiers had angled off to the northeast. Whatever tracks they thought they'd found would only lead them into the middle of the high plains and a whole lot of lonesome. Slocum hated to attribute good things to Jesse James but had to now. Whoever had laid the false trail had done a damned good job of it.

"Where?"

Slocum thought on this, then decided to head for the cave where Jesse had shown him the Knights of the Golden Circle coded message. That was as close to a rendezvous point as he knew. He headed due west toward the mountains, Zeke obediently following with his remuda of stolen horses. By sundown they were in rugged country, and by midnight Slocum reached the winding path leading to the cave. He saw fresh spoor along the trail. Jesse wasn't as inclined to hide his trail now because he knew the soldiers were miles away and out of his hair.

"What'd he do with all the guns and ammunition?" Zeke asked.

"Save those questions for Jesse," Slocum said. He had no idea where Frank James and Charlie Dennison had driven the wagons. The gang might have split up into a half-dozen different segments, one leading the pursuing soldiers astray, others taking the stolen wagons with their cargo to a hiding place, and others heading to this cave.

"I don't see that more 'n two or three riders came this way recently."

Slocum had to agree. Zeke had the makings of a good tracker. But something about one of the hoofprints made Slocum step down, kneel, and run the tips of his fingers over the impression in soft dirt. He lit a lucifer and let the flare die, then held the match close to the print.

"What is it, Slocum?"

"Can't rightly say. This hoofprint was made by a horse shod by a cavalry farrier."

"Think Jesse might have stole a horse or two of his own from the bluecoats?"

Slocum nodded, then mounted. What Zeke said was logical, but it didn't feel right. These tracks were made later than the other two riders on this path. It was nothing more than a guess, but Slocum thought the cavalry horse came by an hour or two later, from the condition of the print and how the mud had dried on the other tracks.

They made their way through the narrow passage and out to the front of the cave, where three horses were tethered. One of them, as Slocum had known, was equipped with a McClelland saddle and other military trappings. He touched the butt of his six-shooter to reassure himself that it rode easy in his holster, then dismounted.

"You think I should stay here?" Zeke asked.

"You cover my back, in case this is a trap," Slocum said. He knew from the voices echoing from inside the cave that it was anything but an ambush. Jesse and Frank laughed and joked with whoever rode the cavalry horse.

"Slocum, wondered when you'd get here."

"You never said where to rendezvous. I figured to come and see if you'd written any new instructions." Slocum pointed toward the chalked-up walls without taking his eyes off the sergeant standing against the far side of the cave.

"He knows the code? You said—"

"Don't let him get under your skin, Berglund," Frank James said. "That's about all he's good for."

"Slocum, meet Sergeant Berglund, command sergeant at Fort Union."

"I saw you earlier," Slocum said. He knew now why the bulk of the horse soldiers had followed the wrong trail. Berglund had ordered them after phantom wagons while Frank and Dennison had slipped away and hidden the rifles and other supplies.

"Do tell. Where?"

"Don't tell me you are old buddies?" Jesse waved off Slocum's answer, not that Slocum would have given it. Berglund would figure it out soon enough. He was almost sorry now he hadn't let Zeke go ahead and kill the four soldiers they had trussed up since they were likely in cahoots with Jesse, too.

"We gonna stand around all night or are we gonna do some business?" Frank asked, irritated. "The quicker we get everything going, the sooner we'll be sittin' our asses on governors' chairs."

"Or in a president's office," Berglund said. "You're going to make one hell of a fine president, Jesse."

"And you'll be restored to your rightful command. General of the Army Simon Berglund. How's that sound?"

"Mighty fine, Jesse, mighty fine."

"You were busted in rank," Slocum said.

"So you do know each other," Jesse said. "Simon was a lieutenant colonel, for the Federals, more's the pity, but they saw fit to bust him over a little matter of supplies going to the wrong depot. He's worked his way back to sergeant, but the Federals are wasting his skills. He's a fine tactician—"

"To your even finer strategy," Berglund cut in, letting Jesse bask in some more praise. Slocum saw how it worked. Berglund buttered up the outlaw and would get command of an entire army in return. Or was it more? Other countries, especially those south of the border, had more generals ruling countries than elected politicians. Let Jesse set up his own country and then a coup with the backing of the army would put Berglund in charge.

For all his skill at robbing trains and banks, Jesse was sadly lacking when it came to being devious enough to deal with men like Simon Berglund. At least, Slocum read it that way and nothing being said changed his mind.

"You'll need to help me design my president's uniform. A president has to have a uniform that'll make the people respect him."

"I have several ideas," Berglund said. "We need to get the revolution started before that's a concern. Where do you have the rifles cached?"

"About two miles from here," Frank James said. "With the armament we took earlier, that makes five hundred rifles, two mountain howitzers, and all the powder, shot, and ammunition we need for the lot."

"Colonel Loebe is still fuming over losing them. I convinced him the guns fell into the Pecos River and were lost. He won't expect them to be aimed at his nose."

"When is all this revolution supposed to start?" Slocum asked.

"Details," Jesse said, waving him to silence. "We need to get more men for the army. General Berglund will take care of that for us, won't you, Simon?"

Slocum saw that Jesse wanted to puff up Berglund's vanity but that it didn't work. This put Slocum on guard. Berglund played a different game and Jesse didn't realize that.

"When you get me the gold, I'll get you the soldiers." Berglund looked hard at Slocum. "Not all the soldiers at Fort Union are happy about their roles. The officers are tyrants and other noncoms think more about putting their men in the stocks than they do in training."

"All your men are well trained?"

"Of course they are, Slocum. You hush up. We have some details to work out. The general and I need to arrange for the Knights of the Golden Circle to assume power smoothly once the revolt is over."

"Fighting is one thing, governing is another."

Slocum said nothing. Whatever he found out would have to be used fast if the sergeant was being handed the gold to bribe the soldiers at the fort.

"He should come with us," Berglund said unexpectedly.

"We don't need him. The two of us can handle what's necessary," Jesse James said.

"The world will know soon enough."

"All right," Jesse said, scowling. "You heard the general. Get in the saddle, Slocum. We're riding out immediately."

Slocum wondered what the sergeant had in mind, but it wouldn't be pleasant. He nodded, considering that this might be a good time for him to just ride off. But the Siren's song of the gold proved too much to escape. It had been years since he'd seen more than a double eagle. A couple gold bars would go a ways toward putting him in the clover.

"You going, Slocum?" Zeke came over. "You want I should ride with you?"

"Stay here," Slocum said. "I'll be back before you know it."

Zeke started to say something more, but Jesse and Berglund came from the cave. The young outlaw stepped back and watched as the three men rode from the cave. Slocum heard Frank James come out and bark orders. The last thing he heard as he wove in and out through the rocks forming the trail was Frank ordering Zeke to bring the captured horses with him when they joined the rest of the gang.

"What's your story?" Berglund asked him. Slocum shrugged. There wasn't a lot to say—there wasn't a lot he wanted to say to any soldier willing to betray his country for a pile of gold.

"Slocum isn't much of a talker, General. But he's solid as a rock. We rode together during the war."

"At Lawrence," Slocum said. Jesse grinned, thinking he had finally won that argument.

"He'll make a good addition to the officer corps. He was a captain."

"C.S.A.?"

"Of course he was a reb," Jesse said. "He wouldn't ride with the Federals. Never against his own people."

Slocum marveled that Jesse didn't see the trouble brewing under his nose. He valued loyalty to the cause above all else and yet he trusted Berglund to turn his loyalty around for the price of a bar or two of gold.

"We need to scout the approaches to the fort," Jesse went on. "We'll sneak a few men into the fort, join up with the soldiers willing to support us and then take over. There won't be more 'n a shot or two fired before the entire post is ours."

"Why not just put sentries on duty to ignore us as we ride up?" Slocum asked.

"I'm not sure the officer of the day will be with us or against us. He's a shavetail lieutenant and full of himself. He thinks he has a career with the Army." Berglund's bitterness boiled out.

Jesse and Berglund discussed matters in a whisper Slocum couldn't overhear. He gave up trying and studied the land around the fort. Stands of trees down by a river formed a weak spot in the perimeter defenses. That Fort Union was more a supply post than one actively fighting the Indians was apparent.

"You wait here," Jesse said when they came within sight of the fort's palisades wall. "I'll be back before you know it."

"Don't go thrashing around in the brush," Berglund warned. "The guards are trained to shoot at anything out of the ordinary."

"I won't move a muscle," Slocum promised.

Jesse James and the sergeant circled the wall to enter through a gate on the south side of the fort. Slocum became increasing edgy when Jesse didn't return within a half hour. The possibility existed that Sergeant Berglund played a different game. He might be a loyal soldier and content with letting the famous outlaw ride into the fort as his prisoner. A medal and a promotion might be in the offing for such a feat.

Slocum paced like a caged animal, trying to find the right angle to study the problem of the Union sergeant's treason. He might be what he claimed or he could be playing a deeper game that would see Jesse and all his gang locked up in the stockade.

A sound made Slocum freeze, his hand went to his six-shooter but he never drew. Something hard and heavy crashed into the back of his skull and he pitched forward, unconscious.

8

Slocum rolled over on a clump of weeds. His head felt like it would split apart and the buzzing in his ears didn't come from insects, though he felt some crawling across his face. From the position of the sun warm against his back it was probably late afternoon, though it might have been early morning. He had no idea how long he had been unconscious.

His belly hurt, and he thought he knew why. He heard his mare whinny a few yards away. He had been tossed belly-down across the saddle and brought here. Wherever here was.

". . . not supposed to just leave him. You heard what the sergeant said."

"To hell with that. He coulda killed us and didn't."

"So we leave him out here to die of thirst? Better to just shoot him, like Sergeant Berglund said."

The argument raged on, giving Slocum a chance to clear his head. He found himself lying on his side, hands bound behind his back. Blinking dirt from his eyes, he saw his horse and the distant sky turning dark at the horizon. From the temperature of the ground, he thought it was getting on to twilight and that he was facing east. All that didn't seem important compared to everything else, but it was all he could grasp mentally. His thoughts were a jumble and he knew he was in a powerful lot of trouble, no matter what the arguing soldiers did.

"We can take his horse back," the first soldier insisted. "It'll fetch a good price in Las Vegas."

"I'm no horse thief."

"You gotta fish or cut bait," the first soldier insisted. "We were told to get rid of him and we did. Nothing was said about his horse."

"He saved our lives. He had the four of us dead to rights. He could have shot us or slit our throats, but he didn't. He tied us up instead."

"And we caught extra duty for a month, too," grumbled the obstinate soldier. "We'd have been better off if he'd done killed us. Now all we'll get out of Berglund is scut duty."

"Better that than being dead."

"All right, all right, let's leave him, though it'd be a mercy to put a bullet in his head. He'll die out here for sure."

"If he gets out of his ropes, he'll hightail it and never be seen again in these parts."

"And if he doesn't, he's a dead man. Either way Berglund don't need to know what happened. But the horse . . ."

The sound of steady hoofbeats leaving him convinced Slocum he was all alone out on the prairie. This wasn't hard desert like farther south. High plains. But it would be mighty cold in nothing flat when the sun at his back faded. He rolled over and stared at the darkening sky. Grunting, he sat up, hands still bound behind his back. Wobbling about, he got his senses about him and struggled to his feet.

"Don't go running off," he said to his mare. The horse looked up, one huge brown eye turned in his direction. He knew the look. If he took even a step forward, she would bolt and he'd be left in the middle of nowhere. Inching toward the horse, shuffling, turning, and making it seem that he intended to do anything but grab the reins, he approached to within a pace.

The horse reared, then ran off to the west, leaving him on foot.

Slocum cursed as he started after the horse. The mare would run a mile or less and then find more grass to crop, giving him another chance to grab the reins. If he failed, he wasn't likely to have another chance. The wind was whipping up and carried a chill to it along with the definite hint of rain from the higher elevations in the mountains. There was no way in hell he could hope to run down a horse in a rainstorm. This part of the country didn't see just rain. Here, when it rained, it *rained*. The arroyos would run full and anyone trapped out in it would be soaked clear through, then frozen when the wind kicked up enough. With hands secured behind his back, he had even less chance of surviving the night.

As he stumbled along, his head cleared up. He felt the goose-egg-sized knot on the back of his skull where he had been struck. He was glad that he had something to show for his lack of caution. He had thought that, if anyone doublecrossed him, it would be Jesse James, not the cavalry sergeant, because he had never thought Berglund would have the opportunity. Two of the soldiers whose lives he had spared had spared his after being ordered to kill him.

Berglund was willing to murder one of Jesse's men. That told Slocum the sergeant was willing to do the same with the outlaw as soon as the gold was in hand.

As he walked, Slocum felt his hands go numb. Then his forearms and his shoulders began to ache and finally everything hurt as if they'd been dipped in fire. He had to get free of the ropes cutting into his wrists. There didn't seem to be an easy way of severing the ropes so he decided on a hard one. He dropped to his knees and reached back and down so he could feel the rowels on his spurs. They were blunted on the tips, but the brace on the side of the spur always got nicked and developed rough spots. Slocum filed them down whenever he had a chance, but that had been weeks ago.

He felt, cut his finger on a sharp section, and then shoved the rope around his wrists down on this section of the spur. If he thought the pain in his shoulders had been fierce before, now he became woozy from the intensity. Forcing himself to rock back and forth, to keep the rope against the ragged edge of the spur, not to black out. He worked for what seemed an eternity and then could take no more. He collapsed forward.

It took him a few seconds to realize he had caught himself before he smashed his face into the parched ground. He moved his arms around. They felt like deadened meat clubs. His wrists bled, but the ropes had been cut through. For once his lack of attention to his gear had saved his life. Slocum rubbed his wrists, flexed his fingers to return circulation, and then got back to his feet.

He had solved one problem but still had to find his horse. Stars popped out in the nighttime sky and the fresh wind against his face rejuvenated him. Then he saw the stars slowly being hidden under a heavy blanket of storm clouds moving off the Sangre de Cristo Mountains, and the heavy odor of impending rain grew heavier in his nostrils.

The darkness prevented him from finding a rise and looking out to find where his horse had gotten off to. He doubted the mare would run far, but the dark worked against him. Still, he would not stop even if he had to walk all the way to Las Vegas. He had a score to settle and not with the two soldiers. He considered himself even with them. He could have killed them and hadn't. They had returned the favor.

His bone to pick was with Sergeant Simon Berglund.

A half hour later, he heard horses ahead. Horses. Several. Along with those sounds came metallic clanking and the creak of wood. Slocum walked faster and saw a man sitting in the back of a wagon feeding a carrot to a horse.

His horse.

"Who's there?" The man jumped down, reached for a rifle, and swung around to cover Slocum as he came closer.

"Somebody who's mighty grateful," Slocum said. "You found my horse."

"I found this here horse wanderin' alone without nobody ridin' her," the man said. "How do I know the horse is yours?"

"I could tell you what's in the saddlebags."

The man looked at him suspiciously.

"Not a whole lot of different things a man carries there."

"There's a Colt Navy wrapped in oilcloth," Slocum said. His holster was empty. The soldiers might not have stolen his horse but they had taken his sidearm. He carried a spare in his gear. "And a shirt with blood on the front."

"That could be anybody's," the man said reluctantly, not wanting to surrender a find like the mare, even in the face of such proof of ownership. "What happened to you?"

"A snake," Slocum said, deciding a lie was more believable than what had really happened. "My mare reared and threw me. I've been trying to catch up with her before the storm hits."

"You noticed that?"

"Hard not to," Slocum said. "There. I was just hit with a raindrop."

"You was?" The man turned toward the mountains and lifted his face to the wind. Slocum closed the distance between them in four quick strides, grabbed the rifle, and wrested it from the man's grip.

"Don't kill me, mister. I ain't got nuthin' in the wagon you'd want."

"The horse *is* mine, and I'm not going to rob you." Slocum went to the mare, rummaged in the saddlebags, and found his spare six-shooter. He took time to load it and get it settled into his holster. Only then did he toss the rifle back to the teamster.

"You've givin' me back my rifle?"

"I'd give you a reward for finding my horse, but I'm flat broke," Slocum said. He had a few dollars in his pocket, but the teamster had tried to keep the horse. Slocum didn't feel too obligated to pony up a reward, but with his six-gun at his side again, he was in better spirits. The freighter wasn't going to suffer any at Slocum's hand now, unless he tried to do something really stupid like steal the mare.

"Glad to be of help," the man said. He looked back into the sky. "Don't feel no rain."

"Not yet," Slocum said, "but it's coming. There's one hell of a storm on its way." He swung into the saddle and rode toward Las Vegas without another word.

The rain began fitfully pelting him with huge drops, and by the time he rode into Las Vegas, the storm was in full force. Head down, hat brim pulled to protect his face, he sought the boardinghouse where Audrey had said she rented a room. Only one house looked to fill the bill. Slocum rode around back and put his horse in a small stable. He had guessed right about this being the proper place since Audrey's horse occupied the only other stall. As much as he wanted to rush to the house, he took time to dry his horse, feed her, and then tend his gear to keep it functional.

Only then did he run across the yard, already ankle deep in mud, to the house. The adobe had been constructed in typical Spanish fashion, with a high wall surrounding the house. To get into the courtyard he would have had to open the gate. A quick jiggle of the handle showed it was locked. The woman renting rooms didn't want nighttime visitors to her patrons.

Slocum circled the mud wall, found a spot that had begun to collapse and needed repair, jumped, caught the crumbling edge, and pulled himself over. He flipped around in midair and landed in a garden. He hoped he didn't do too much damage as he carefully stepped to a flagstone path. By the time he reached the house situated in the middle of the compound, the rain had erased his boot prints.

The windows were narrow, and it took him some time to work around to the wing holding the bedrooms. He peered in one window after another and found only empty rooms. The fifth room, however, had a blouse laid out on the bed that Slocum recognized as Audrey's. He rattled the window, got it open in spite of its latch, and ducked inside.

Barely had he stepped into the room when he heard voices outside in the hall.

"I tell you, Sheriff, that's who it is. There's a hefty reward on his head."

"This your room?"

"I don't think Señora Gonzales would mind if you came in for a moment. But only a moment." The door creaked open, giving Slocum a quick glimpse at Audrey blocking the door and a tall, thin man behind her. He couldn't get back out the window in time. He grabbed the wardrobe door and opened it. A few of Audrey's dresses hung inside. He knew they were hers by the distinctive odor. He pulled the door shut just as she and the lawman came into the room.

"I'll leave the door open, ma'am, so there won't be any problem."

"I don't think there will be."

Slocum held his breath when he heard the click of Audrey's shoes approaching the wardrobe. He clung to the edge of the door with his fingertips, unable to close it. She started to open it, then turned and spoke to the sheriff.

"I have the wanted poster in my bag." She crossed the room, rummaged under the bed, and pulled out the bag. After taking out a stack of wanted posters, she laid one on the bed and pointed. "This is the man, Sheriff. There's a hundred-dollar reward on his head."

"Don't reckon I've seen him around."

"He's riding with the James Gang. I saw him a day or so back."

"A hundred dollars is a fine prize for him," the sheriff said. "You don't have the look of a bounty hunter. Are you sure you want to do this?"

"I'm sure I can get in good with him and lure him into your capable hands."

"The town marshal's a good man. Why do you want me to help out?"

"I . . . I approached him. He wanted half the reward."

"So he'd take half while you took all the risk?" The sheriff laughed heartily. "That's Jay Hooker, all right. He'd steal the buttons off a dead man's vest if he thought he could get away with it. Even if he didn't much need the buttons."

"You'll help me capture this desperado?"

"Any reason you think I wouldn't ask for half the reward, too?"

Slocum heard Audrey suck in her breath. He held the door shut but saw her moving about now and again through the narrow crack between door and wardrobe. For two cents he would have kicked open the door, drawn, and shot both her and the sheriff. The sheriff wasn't acting as if the wanted poster she had shown him was anyone special. It certainly wasn't Jesse or Frank James or the lawman would have commented on that.

"Someone riding with the James Gang," she had said. Slocum began to fume. She was thinking on turning him over to the law for the reward on his head. He had thought she was confused as to what she was doing. Bounty hunter or treasure hunter or reporter. They had all sounded like pipe dreams to him, but Audrey had a better developed sense of her goal than he'd thought. She might want the gold, but she wasn't going to pass up the chance at a bounty on his head.

Although Slocum couldn't see the wanted poster, it had to be the one on him for killing the federal judge back in Georgia. The amount was right and the poster crackled and crinkled, yellow and brittle from age. It wasn't anything she had come across recently.

"You can get yourself killed. From what this says, the man's a bloodthirsty killer."

"I don't know about that," she said. "He's got a strong chin and looks rather noble, in a barbaric way."

The sheriff laughed harshly. Slocum saw him poke his finger down on the poster, breaking off a corner.

"You make one mistake with a man like this and he'll gun you down and never show a bit of remorse, 'cept for wasting a bullet. He might not even shoot you, if you follow my meaning."

"I understand how dangerous this will be, Sheriff. You do, too."

"My posse's been scouring the countryside for these owlhoots and they've stayed one step ahead of us for weeks now. The gang stole two wagons loaded with guns and ammunition. I don't have to tell you what mischief they can get into with that kind of firepower."

"Bringing this one to justice might be like pulling a thread on a piece of cloth. Tug enough on him and the whole fabric might come unraveled."

"That chin you were admirin' so," the sheriff said, "tells me he's boastful and arrogant and would likely die before givin' up the rest of the gang." He heaved a deep sigh. "The only reason I'm not runnin' you out of the territory to keep you from tryin' this, Miss Underwood, is that I want Jesse James so bad I can taste it. He's been comin' here on and off to hide out for a couple years. The sheriff 'fore me looked the other way."

"You're a better lawman than that."

"I'm not scared of Jesse James or his brother, but this one has the look of a mad dog killer to him. You might kill him, but he's not gonna give up his partners."

"I can be very persuasive, Sheriff." Audrey shuffled the wanted posters into a stack and returned them to her bag before shoving it back under the bed.

"I'm sure," the lawman said. "I'm sure you can, Miss Underwood. I'd better be going now 'fore the señora starts wonderin' what kinda business we're doin'."

"I'll see you out," Audrey said.

Slocum waited a few seconds, then chanced a quick peek around the wardrobe door. Audrey and the lawman had left. He stepped from the wardrobe and noticed that he had left wet footprints on the floor. How either the sheriff or Audrey had missed those, he couldn't say. They were too busy arranging to put his neck in a noose.

He chanced a quick look out into the hallway and saw Audrey, her back to him, shaking hands with the sheriff to seal their treacherous deal. Slocum closed the door, went to the window, and opened it. In seconds he was out in the rain once more, over the adobe wall, and mounted, riding into the storm to find a safe, warm place to sleep the night.

The stable in town wasn't Audrey's bed, as he had anticipated, but he felt safer surrounded by the horses. They weren't likely to turn him in for a reward.

9

Slocum stared at the markings on the cave wall but couldn't make head nor tail of them. He knew the general scheme of the code, but without a book with the symbols deciphered, there wasn't any way to be sure what he was seeing. He reached out and traced over the new chalk marks, as if touching them would somehow give him insight into their meaning.

It almost did. He felt as if the meaning was at the tip of his tongue—the tip of his finger. He identified one symbol that had to mean gold and the numbers surrounding it gave the location of the hoard Jesse James had hidden to be used as a bribe. Slocum knew the reason this was newly added— the gold would be moved to a spot where Simon Berglund could get to it, supposedly to bribe other soldiers at Fort Union.

"You disappeared," came a soft voice. Slocum spun, his six-shooter out and aimed. He had his thumb on the hammer and came within an inch of drawing it back and letting it drop on a round.

"I didn't hear you ride up," Slocum said.

"I saw your horse and thought it might be one of the gang," Audrey Underwood said, coming into the cave. For a brief moment she was delightfully silhouetted by the light outside, then moved to a spot where she could look at the chalk code. "I didn't want to tangle with them, but when I saw it was your mare, I knew it was all right. Where'd you go?"

She wasn't acting as if she had shown his wanted poster to the sheriff the night before. Slocum had seen how good an actress she could be, and it hardly seemed likely she was able to hide her real plan from him. He saw no hint of betrayal in her bright eyes.

"I scouted around the countryside and saw the sheriff riding out. What's his name?"

"Sheriff Narvaiz," she said without hesitation or even a hint of guile. "He's much smarter than his deputy. From what I can tell, the sheriff has sent his deputy and most of the posse back to sit and wait for his word to assemble again."

"Do tell."

"What's wrong, John? You're acting strangely."

"New symbols. I think Jesse has moved the gold and is getting ready to spring his revolt on the territory. Does this mean anything to you?"

Audrey came over, bent low to look at the symbol, and Slocum caught her scent. He remembered it well from hiding in the wardrobe the night before—and from earlier times with her. She was inches away, her back to him as if she trusted him completely.

"You're mighty confident," he said.

"No, not really. I think I know what it means but can't be sure. This is similar to a symbol Jesse used in a cave back in Kansas."

"I mean hobnobbing with the sheriff like you did."

"I'm trying to get a line on others in the gang. Taking Jesse on straightaway won't get us anywhere. He's avoided too many lawmen up till now, so I decided to come at him from a different direction."

"What's that?"

"The men riding with him all have wanted posters on them. If I can lay a trap for one of them and let Sheriff Narvaiz capture him, this might lead us to not only the gold but also to capturing Jesse and all the rest."

"Who did you have in mind?"

"Since you're not doing such a good job with them, I decided to try someone else."

"What do you mean?" Slocum rested his hand on his Colt Navy again. Audrey didn't turn but worked her way down the row of symbols, then backtracked going from right to left.

"This might be it. They wrote their code backward. Do you know of a saddle pass anywhere nearby? This symbol is the sun and those numbers are something about the time of day, but I can't tell what."

"Saddle pass? There's one not two miles from here to the south."

"South? Well, that might be so. If they reversed everything else, it might be a key because it looks like this means to the north."

"Time of day," Slocum said, distracted from Audrey's betrayal because of the lure of the gold. "That'd have to mean during the daylight hours. It gets dark faster close to the mountains."

"My guess would be noon, or an hour before or after. These are new ciphers for me, but Jesse can't get too fancy or whoever he's dealing with won't understand."

"He's trying to bribe a soldier who's mighty sharp," Slocum said.

"Still, shall we find this pass and see—" Audrey turned and ran smack into Slocum. She looked at him and tried to step back, only to find herself pinned to the wall by his body. "John, there's not much time. It's after ten. If we want to study the pass an hour before and after noon, we ought to start if it's two miles away."

"Yeah," he said.

"You're acting peculiar. What's wrong?"

"Let's ride," he said. If he had a lick of sense, he'd toss Audrey into the pit and then ride like hell to get out of New Mexico Territory before Jesse stirred up things. He could always come back this way after it all spilled over because he didn't believe anyone could wrest an entire country from the government in Washington. They had finished a war to keep the entire country intact. Holding on to New Mexico Territory would be far easier for them, no matter what politicians worked against continued union.

But the gold. Jesse had to have a mountain of gold to bribe even a fair number of the soldiers at the fort. They weren't paid much, but they were mostly war veterans who didn't know any other job. The few recruits were the lowest paid but might actually have a touch of patriotism in their bones. No matter how many—or how few—of the soldiers Jesse thought to bribe, it had to amount to several thousand dollars that would ride more easily in John Slocum's saddlebags than in a turncoat's pocket.

Turncoat. Betrayal. Audrey Underwood. He forced himself to keep his hand away from his pistol. If anything, he wanted to strangle her with his bare hands for her betrayal.

"No," she said. "We're not going anywhere until you tell me what's wrong. What did you find while you were out scouting? Did Jesse say something that spooked you?"

He faced her and said, "Who in the gang are you trying to get the sheriff to arrest?"

"I don't dare ask him to go after either Jesse or Frank," she said, pressing her lips together. "That's obvious. If either of them is caught, the other will expend all the money and effort to free his brother from jail. I need a member of the gang who matters to them but for whom they wouldn't risk giving up this cockeyed scheme of rebellion."

"Me?"

Audrey laughed.

"Don't flatter yourself, John. Jesse would as soon shoot you as let you ride with him. He needs guns for his revolt, and you rode with the guerrillas. He thinks he can trust you—just a bit. No, someone closer to him. Charlie Dennison. If I can lure Dennison into a trap and the sheriff can arrest him . . ." Her words trailed off as Slocum laughed. She put her hands on her flaring hips and glowered. "What's so damned funny?"

"You'll never trick Charlie Dennison. Kill him, maybe, but lead him into an ambush? Never."

"I have to try something since you're not doing a thing."

Slocum wondered if she was lying to him about Dennison. It seemed incredible that she couldn't know how vicious the man was. He would as soon kill her as look at her. Slocum had seen men in his day who took greater pleasure in watching their victim die, but not that many. Charlie Dennison was a killer through and through.

"You don't think I am capable of this. I'm telling you, I can be an effective bounty hunter."

"You'd risk your life for a hundred dollars?"

"That's what's offered for Dennison," she said. "How'd you know that?"

Slocum still wasn't sure she hadn't shown his wanted poster to the sheriff but how anyone could lie without revealing so much as a tic or guilty look was beyond him. Audrey might be telling the truth.

But what if she wasn't?

"Just a guess," he said. He guided his horse through the now familiar narrow path and out into a rocky field, headed south. After twenty minutes of riding, he saw the edge of a pass going deeper into the Sangre de Cristo Mountains that was unlike others. This was shallow and rounded rather than having steep, vertical sides.

"That matches what I deciphered," Audrey said, giving

him a sidelong look. Neither had spoken during the ride, Slocum not sure what to say to her and the woman resolutely staring straight ahead as if she could see through rock.

"I don't know if there's anything like it to the north," Slocum said.

"I haven't scouted this area too well."

"What time is it?" She peered up at the sun, poking through heavy clouds that promised more rain later in the day.

Slocum checked his watch, then snapped shut the cover and tucked it away in his vest pocket.

"About noon," he said. "We started later than I'd thought."

Audrey drew rein in the middle of the pass and looked around. Several minutes passed before she said, "I don't see anything that directs us to a cache."

Slocum started to agree when the clouds parted and a ray of sunlight caught two rocky spires on the southernmost side of the pass. A V-shaped shadow was cast. He and Audrey looked at one another. Both smiled. The shadow looked like an arrow pointing toward the far side of the pass.

They rode slowly in the direction, following the gently sloping land until they looked up and saw a rocky overhang.

"It's not a cave but it might serve as a hiding place." Slocum jumped down and scrambled up the rocky slope. To his surprise by the time he reached the rocky ledge, Audrey was there waiting for him.

"I found a trail—a well-traveled trail," she said. "Looked as if horses went up and down it recently."

Slocum saw the trail curling down back toward the bottom of the pass. In his haste, he had not investigated very well. Worse, his rush to find the gold had turned off all logic. If gold had been hidden here, Jesse and the rest of his gang wouldn't have struggled up the rocky slope carrying the bullion. Or did they store gold coins in leather sacks? The golden lure had dazzled him and left him vulnerable.

He felt a curious itch in the middle of his back. If Audrey had been dickering with Sheriff Narvaiz about turning him in, she could have shot him easily at any time while his back was turned to her.

"See where they came?" She stepped to one side and pointed. The rain had washed away much of the hoofprints but enough remained to show more than one horse had come to this point on the side of the pass.

He ducked down and moved rocks until he found a large cavity that had been dug out by hand and lined with stones to keep the sides from caving in.

"What have you found, John? Is the gold there?"

"Empty," he said, crawling back and sitting with his back to a stone face. "But something's been stored here recently."

"Let me look." Audrey dropped to hands and knees to crawl in. Again she showed no hesitation about turning her back on him. He couldn't decide if she was confident that he believed her story about meeting with the sheriff the night before or if she was just too assured to think he would shoot her.

She crawled back and sat beside him.

"You're right. The gold was here not too long ago."

"Something was here," Slocum corrected. "There's nothing to prove Jesse hid gold here. He might have stored a half-dozen crates of rifles or even ammunition."

"It was the gold," she said firmly. "There's no reason for him to unload the wagons with the arms and store them here. He wanted the gold here for a reason."

"From the look of the pass, it's well traveled," Slocum said. "This might be a regular patrol route for the cavalry." His mind raced ahead. This would be a good spot for Berglund to get his payoff. A squad of men might carry the gold back to Fort Union for bribing, as Jesse intended. Or the sergeant might have moved the gold elsewhere, intending to retrieve it later.

Most likely, Berglund had moved the gold and was long

gone. Slocum wondered if the sergeant could run far enough with the gold once Jesse found he had been double-crossed.

"There is only one way the gold might have gone," Audrey said. She stood and looked back eastward, but Slocum knew this wasn't true. If Berglund had the gold, he could have gone through the pass. He wasn't sure where the road at the bottom of the saddle led, but heading toward Taos with a few thousand dollars' worth of gold was a good way to get out of the territory. Head north or south and Jesse or someone in his gang was likely to spot him. East was out of the question for the same reason. The land turned flat and Berglund could be spotted. But west?

Once he got to Taos, he could head north into Colorado or keep pressing on to the west. Depending on how much gold was involved, Berglund could travel fast, find himself a train depot, and be anywhere in the country within weeks.

"Someone's coming," Audrey said. "I see movement, but I can't tell who it is."

Slocum stood, shielded his eyes with his hands, and caught sight of the lead rider.

"It's Jesse and he's got a half-dozen men with him. Chances are good he's coming here."

"He can't find us!" Audrey turned and crashed into him in her haste.

"There's no way we can get back to the road and stay ahead of him," Slocum said. He gauged distances and times. Jesse was coming too fast for them to escape.

For *them* to escape.

He still wondered if Audrey was selling him out to Sheriff Narvaiz, but he saw no way of turning her over to Jesse and having the outcome be good for him. There were too many explanations to be made why he and the woman were poking around in one of the Knights of the Golden Circle caches.

"Keep going. Lead your horse down the side trail. That way!" Slocum pointed.

"But they'll see us."

"I'll decoy him. You get on back to Las Vegas." Slocum almost added, "And fetch the sheriff." He didn't. "I'll meet you there."

"I'm staying in the boardinghouse. Mrs. Gonzales's at the edge of town."

"Go," Slocum said. He was too distracted to return the kiss she gave him before grabbing her horse's reins and taking the trail circling the hillside.

Slocum started down the road to where he'd left his horse. He didn't know what he'd say to Jesse James but he'd think of something. If he didn't come up with something plausible, he was a dead man.

10

"What's he doin' here, Jesse?" Charlie Dennison reached for his six-shooter but got tangled up.

"Whoa, hold your horses, Charlie. There's a good way to find out." Jesse James turned and looked hard at Slocum. "What're you doing here?"

Slocum didn't miss how Jesse had his hand on his own six-gun. There wouldn't be any hesitation if a good answer wasn't offered. The rest of the gang riding behind him also looked a bit confused. That meant Jesse had told them to follow but hadn't said where. They would have thought he was supposed to join them along the trail if Dennison and Jesse hadn't made such a big point of asking what he was hunting for so near their cache.

"There's nothing up there," Slocum said. He didn't bother looking over his shoulder, but both Jesse and Charlie Dennison looked directly at the rock overhang. Nobody else in the gang so much as twitched. Only they knew the location of the cache.

"'Course not, Slocum," said Jesse. "That wasn't what I asked. You want to answer me?"

"I think Berglund is going to double-cross you."

"What gives you that notion?"

Slocum explained how he had been slugged by two soldiers in Berglund's command but didn't elaborate on how he had come to still be alive. He saw that question burned on Dennison's lips, who was willing to finish the job the soldiers had started. Jesse held up his hand to silence his henchman.

"This might just be a misunderstanding. Soldiers get real protective if they see you standing around their fort."

"Where'd you think I got off to?" Slocum asked.

"I figured you had a hankering for a drop of whiskey and went on back to town. When me and Berglund finished our business, I looked for you but Las Vegas was swarming with deputized drunks. The sheriff must have pinned badges on anybody that could stand up straight for more 'n ten seconds. Never saw so many lawmen this side of a Pinkerton convention."

"I believe you," Slocum said.

"What?" Jesse James reared back in surprise. "What do you believe?"

"That you didn't know anything about Berglund wanting me dead and sending his two soldiers out to take care of me. I wish you'd been a bit more curious about why I'd up and ride off like I didn't have a care in the world. I thought you knew me better than that."

Slocum had turned the tables on Jesse and made it seem that the outlaw leader was in the wrong. The best Slocum could tell, Jesse hadn't told Berglund to eliminate an unwanted member of his gang.

Better than this, they had swapped lies back and forth long enough for Audrey to get away. He wished it were easier to determine what game she played. The only way he could be certain was to get a look at the wanted posters stuffed into her bag. If his was there, he would know she was trying to use him as a chip in a bigger poker game with Sheriff Narvaiz and Jesse James as players.

"I need all the men I can rustle up, Slocum. There's no reason for me to have Berglund kill you."

"I know that, Jesse. If you wanted me dead, you'd do it yourself."

Again Slocum caught the outlaw off guard. He started to say something, then laughed heartily.

"Yeah, Slocum, we know each other real good."

"That don't explain why he's here, Jesse. He's *here*." Charlie Dennison had freed his pistol and laid it across the saddle in front of him where he could swing it around and get off a shot or two before Slocum could clear leather. Slocum saw how Dennison hesitated around Jesse. He wasn't likely to let his fiery temper get out of control unless Jesse permitted it.

"The man's got a point, Slocum. Why are you here?"

"I got back to the other cave to see if you left any new message. There were a few symbols I could make out from what you'd said before. They led me here."

"How?" The question escaped Jesse's lips before he could stop it.

"I figured since everything was put down backwards this time, all the instructions were reversed, too. You wrote 'north' so that had to mean south. I read the cipher for 'pass' and this was the best choice, so I came here thinking to find you or more code."

"And you found nothing at all up there?"

"A hollowed-out spot where gold might have been cached," Slocum said, again taking Jesse aback with his honesty. The outlaw had expected him to lie, but Slocum saw no reason. Either Jesse let him live or there'd be one hell of a gunfight. Slocum doubted he would ride away from it, but Jesse and Dennison would be his first victims.

"That's more than I wanted the rest of the boys to hear," Jesse said. "But the gold's never been here. It's closer to Fort Union so moving it when the time comes won't be such a chore. But I'm glad you're here because I'm getting everyone in the gang together for a little raid."

"You can't trust him," Dennison said. "We don't need him. Let me kill him."

"Charlie, shut up. Slocum's a crack shot and mighty fast with that Colt of his, unless I miss my guess. You good, Slocum? Real good?"

The outlaw goaded him, but Slocum refused to give in. He smiled, pulled back his coat to expose the ebony butt of his six-shooter at his left hip, and then squared off.

"Want to find out?"

"Who you talking to, Slocum? Me or Charlie?" Jesse was amused now. Slocum doubted there would be any gunplay but didn't relax. He watched Charlie Dennison closely for the slightest sign the owlhoot would lift his pistol. He saw how Dennison kept his thumb on the hammer, ready to draw it back and get off the first shot. A flicker of doubt clouded his eyes, and Slocum knew he had him. Before this moment, Dennison figured he could gun down his foe, but the time had passed. He doubted his ability to lift and fire before Slocum could get to his six-shooter in its cross-draw holster and send a bullet winging his way.

"Put your gun away, Charlie. And you, Slocum, mount up. We're riding on through to the other side of the pass to a town called Encantado. What do you know about it?"

"Nothing," Slocum admitted. He tugged at his horse's reins so he could mount without turning his back on Dennison. Seeing such caution, Dennison slammed his six-gun back into its holster. If looks could kill, Dennison would be spitting out death like a Gatling gun.

"You still got a spare pistol, like you did when we rode with Quantrill?"

Slocum shook his head, remembering his other six-shooter had been stolen by the soldiers who had bushwhacked him.

"Charlie, give him a spare. You got plenty."

"Jesse, I—"

"Do it." His voice carried a steel bite to it, telling Slocum that Dennison had been kicking up a fuss and this was Jesse's way of establishing who was in charge.

Slocum silently took the pistol Charlie passed over and tucked it into his belt. He knew then what the gang was going to do and it didn't set well with him.

"We won't have to do more than hurrah the place," Jesse explained. "There might be some resistance but not much. I picked this as the place to start because it was isolated and yet on the road through the mountains. We can control the freighters as they go from Las Vegas to Taos."

"We'll charge 'em a tariff," Dennison said. "This will be our country's first source of income."

"How do you intend to hold the town?"

"Encantado doesn't have much of a population and no marshal to get in the way. If they have any trouble, they call on the cavalry over at Fort Union."

Slocum began to see the way the plot was fitting together. Berglund was supposed to send only men loyal to the Knights of the Golden Circle or maybe only those who weren't. Riding into a sleepy mountain town, expecting only a few drunk cowboys and finding the James Gang in charge would be quite a shock—and one the troops wouldn't be ready for. He remembered that Frank had mentioned having a couple mountain howitzers.

As he rode, he studied the higher ground. A single field piece could command this pass, giving that much more authority to the claim of a new country.

"You want the cavalry sent?" Slocum asked.

"You got it all figured out," Dennison said. "You tell us."

Slocum explained the ways he saw it, both with troops loyal to the uprising and those unsuspecting.

"See, Charlie, Slocum's got a head on his shoulders. We want the troops that aren't loyal so we can get rid of them."

"And leave those that are loyal to you back at the fort so you can seize it from within."

"I ought to have you doing my planning," Jesse said,

laughing. "This is going to be great fun. By the end of the year, we'll all be governing our own separate states and the Golden Circle will be forged. There're uprisings in Mexico and Central America planned. From this we can sail on over to the Caribbean and take those islands, completing the circle. You ever been on a sailing ship, Slocum?"

"Can't say that I have."

"Me neither. Might be fun to lead a marine invasion of Cuba or one of them other islands. I hear tell them local folks are swimming in rum and smoking the best damned cigars anywhere. The señoritas roll the best cigars against their naked thighs. A sight to behold. Or so I'm told."

"If I can't ride there, I don't want to go," Slocum said. He saw several riders approaching from the north, just as they started down the slope on the far side of the pass. Ahead he saw a small town of a few dozen adobe buildings. Hornos were filled with baking bread and the people went about their lives, unaware of the tide about to wash over them.

"Reinforcements," Jesse said when Slocum spotted the riders. "We got damned near fifty men in our little army, and when the gold is swapped, we'll quadruple that, with more 'n a hundred all trained soldiers."

"Don't trust Berglund," Slocum warned. He wanted to sow the seeds of discord, but he shouldn't have said a word to the outlaw leader. Let him find that Berglund was a sidewinder about ready to strike. The more confusion in the outlaw ranks, the better it was.

And the better chance Slocum had of finding the gold and making off with at least some of it in the confusion.

"Don't go givin' Jesse advice. He's got everything planned out all good and proper." Dennison grated his teeth together as he spoke. His festering anger was barely held in check. Slocum considered pushing him over the edge but Jesse interrupted.

"I do not, indeed, need any advice at this moment," Jesse James said. He drew his pistol and fired it once into the air.

The newcomers rode to his signal and the small army massed a mile from Encantado.

Slocum let his horse sidestep away and go to the edge of the gathered army. He didn't want to ride into this town, shooting innocent men and women the way he had during the war, but if he didn't, Charlie Dennison would be on him in an instant. As Jesse began addressing the men, whipping them into a killing frenzy, Slocum wondered if Audrey had gotten back to Las Vegas yet. If she contacted Sheriff Narvaiz, that might derail Jesse's battle plan. The sheriff was likely to bring along a posse. With the resistance to be expected from the men in Encantado, the outlaws would find themselves caught between the law and the citizens.

It wouldn't be the first time for Jesse and the others to be in such a situation. They'd probably escape, but the wild-ass scheme to forge a new country out of New Mexico Territory would be ended. That might be worth the deaths of a few of the townspeople because it would prevent even worse killings in the future.

"Any chance we'll be facing any of the cavalry?" Slocum asked.

"You hush up, Slocum. This is going according to my plan. There won't be any bluecoats down there. Not a one. Everybody! Guns ready?"

A cheer went up. Slocum drew the spare six-shooter he had been given, cocked it, and considered how hard it would be to accidentally—on purpose—cut down Charlie Dennison during the fight.

Before he had a chance to position himself so he could ride near Jesse's henchman, a shot rang out and the entire gang moved as one, save for Slocum. His horse reared before joining the throng rushing downward toward Encantado.

The people in the town must have had some small hint that a whole lot of hurt was washing down over them. Slocum saw several men duck indoors and come out with rifles. They started shooting before any of Jesse's gang was in range. The men wasted their shots—and then their lives were wasted. The front of the onslaught hit the main street with the force of a hundred pounds of dynamite exploding. Jesse and Charlie rode side by side, Jesse shooting at everyone on his left side and Dennison on his right. Slocum saw no fewer than six men sag under the leaden onslaught.

Jesse James had practiced this maneuver more times than Slocum wanted to think. He put his heels to his horse and shot forward, but he held back shooting. He rode hard and drew closer to Charlie Dennison. If anyone in this town died, it ought to be him. Slocum leveled the pistol the outlaw had given him and judged the motion of his own galloping horse and that which Dennison rode the best he could. He got the man's broad back in his sights and fired.

Slocum let out a screech as the six-gun misfired in his grip. Pieces of hot metal flew in all directions. One piece of shrapnel cut Slocum's cheek like a hot knife. Another burned a hole through the brim of his hat. Other than this, his face was untouched. He had seen guns blow up and blind the marksman—or worse. Hands could be blown off or lives lost.

He kept riding, clutching the useless gun in his hand. Blood oozed out from around charred skin where pieces of the barrel had blown straight back and burned him.

Slocum was aware of the resistance fading throughout Encantado. The men threw down their rifles and held their hands high over their heads. A few of them died as Jesse's excited gang couldn't find a way to lasso in their bloodlust. A second pass through the town, then a street-by-street hunt quickly brought everyone outdoors and into the plaza.

Jesse rode his horse into the gazebo and turned it slowly, horseshoes clomping drum-loud on the wood floor. He grinned ear to ear at the quick conquest of the sleepy town.

"What happened to you, Slocum?" Jesse James called.

"The damned gun Dennison gave me blew up in my hand."

"You better get that tended to. It looks mighty bad."

"Feels worse," Slocum said. He plucked a few metal

splinters from his forearm and the fleshy part of his thumb. Letting it bleed to clean out any infection produced what appeared to be a bloody stump at the end of his right arm.

"You lose something, Slocum?" Charlie Dennison rode over and sneered at him. "Might be you won't have to kill anybody again. That'd suit a coward like you, wouldn't it?"

"Next time, I won't use your gun," Slocum said.

Before Dennison could snap back, Jesse fired three quick shots through the roof of the gazebo.

"Reckon you folks will have to repair those holes before it rains again. But then you're alive and able to repair your homes and your lives, thanks to me. I'm Jesse James and I just liberated you from the U.S. government."

His men cheered. The townspeople remained silent. If anything they huddled together more, seeking reassurance from their family and neighbors that they would not suffer the fate a dozen or more in Encantado already had.

"First off, you don't bury none of the bodies. You let them get real ripe in the hot sunlight to remind you of what you're leaving behind. As soon as I can, I'll bring in supplies for a big feast to celebrate the opening shots of a rebellion that'll bring about the Kingdom of the Golden Circle."

"Cheer, damn you!" shouted Dennison. When only a few men did so, Dennison shot two men glowering at him. "Cheer your conqueror. Cheer for your new freedom from them damned Yankees!"

This produced more of a response. Slocum guessed not everyone in Encantado was pleased with paying taxes to a distant government. They had seen how brutal the new regime might be, but it was close at hand, not two thousand miles away in a place they had never seen.

"We're gonna set up a ruling council. At the head of the new council will be this man, Charlie Dennison. He'll appoint members to the council from your rank. Y'all will rule yourselves from now on."

Slocum held his breath. The people of Encantado would

rule themselves as long as Charlie Dennison and ultimately Jesse James allowed them to do so. The ones most vocal about supporting their new rulers would move up fast and find themselves in positions of power. Those that opposed Jesse would join the dozen already killed.

"Right now, get on back to work. You'll be told when the council meeting will be held." Jesse fired his pistol again until it came up empty. Then he rode out of the gazebo and stopped beside Dennison and Slocum.

"Charlie, you know what's got to be done. We have to be certain the cavalry sent out here's who we think. Then you can set about finding the men who'll support us on the ruling council." Jesse took a deep breath, closed his eyes, and tipped his head back to bask in the sun like a lizard. "Yes, sir, this is the first baby step toward taking over the whole damn territory."

Slocum pressed his bandanna into his wounds but never took his eyes off Jesse. If the pistol hadn't blown up in his hand, he would have been smart to take out not only Dennison but the outlaw leader, too.

Jesse opened his eyes and stared hard at Slocum.

"This is the first town. But there'll be more in a hurry. We got to move fast so we can consolidate our power. What town would you like, Slocum?" Before he got an answer, Jesse went on. "Santa Fe. You can rule over Santa Fe. We'll need somebody with a strong hand to control there since there's a train depot in Lamy. We wouldn't want the blue-coats to bring in reinforcements and outflank us before we got control of Fort Union. Yes, we need a strong hand there." He stared at Slocum's injured hand and laughed.

If Slocum could have held his Colt, Jesse James would have been a dead man.

11

"This is the life," Zeke said, boots hiked up to the table top and a bottle of whiskey in his hand. He took another long pull on it and offered it to Slocum.

The whiskey was bitter and left an aftertaste in Slocum's mouth. Or maybe it was the way Jesse James had taken over Encantado that caused the bad taste. He had seen this kind of invasion happen too many times while riding with guerrilla bands. They cowed the citizens of a town, then took whatever they wanted. It wasn't any different from being a train robber, but Slocum felt it was dirtier somehow. It certainly left him feeling like he needed a bath—and he knew no amount of scrubbing could ever wipe away what he felt.

"Dennison seems like he's been ready to be mayor of a town for all his life," Slocum said.

"I'm gettin' me one, too. Jesse promised. Not right away, but soon."

"Where's he going next?"

"Someplace bigger's my guess. He didn't tell me. He plays those cards real close to his vest." Zeke took another

102

drink and balanced the bottle on the edge of the table, where it teetered and then fell. He paid no attention to it but yelled, "Bartender! Bring us another bottle. This one's empty."

Slocum saw the suppressed fury on the barkeep's face, but the man brought a new bottle and put it on the table, just an inch beyond Zeke's reach.

"You and Dennison getting to be partners?" Slocum asked. "Seems like you're admiring what he does more and more."

"He knows what he's doing. Him and Jesse are tight. You could do worse than to be like Charlie, too. But then you know Jesse and he's promised you the chance to be governor of an entire state." Zeke heaved a sigh, strained, and got the bottle into his grip. "Governor. That's what I want to be."

"Not president?"

"Jesse's claimed that for himself."

"When a country's formed like this, a coup isn't that unusual," Slocum said.

"You thinkin' on overthrowing Jesse? That's mighty bold, Slocum."

"Just pointing out that hitching your wagon to the wrong star might bring you crashing down to earth."

Zeke laughed, drank a little more, and then dropped his feet to the floor with a thud. He leaned forward and tried to keep his voice down to a whisper. He didn't succeed.

"Jesse's the right star, and I know how to drive wagons and throw a diamond hitch on a pack mule. I never amounted to much and my pa always beat me and said I'd never amount to a hill of beans. This'll show 'em. Why, I might end up as mayor of Taos."

"Taos?"

"Yeah, sure, why not? I heard Jesse say he'd start you out in Santa Fe 'fore letting you work up to governor. Don't know how he's gonna cut out the state but maybe me and you, we can be governors of adjoining states."

"Might happen," Slocum said. He knew Jesse was promising all his gang positions of power and hinting that along with such titles would come the spoils. There wasn't a one of them who knew the first thing about running a town, much less an entire state or a country. The lure of being able to steal legally was more than any of the outlaws could resist.

"Damned right. It *will* happen," Zeke said.

"Hey, Slocum, stop getting drunk and come with me."

Slocum looked up. Jesse James stood in the doorway, the bright sunlight silhouetting him. The urge to draw and fire at such an easy target faded fast when Slocum saw Charlie Dennison and Frank James behind Jesse.

"El presidente wants you," Zeke said, a hint of envy in his voice. "Better not keep him waiting."

"Wouldn't want to do that," Slocum said, heaving to his feet. He spat in the direction of the cuspidor on his way out. The taste in his mouth refused to go away. The bright sun as he stepped into the dusty main street made him squint. He was glad he had resisted cutting Jesse down when he had such an easy target. A half-dozen others from the gang were tightly bunched outside and would have blown him to bloody ribbons if he had killed their leader.

"I need you along to do a little negotiating down south."

"Santa Fe?"

"You'll find out. Get into the saddle."

Dennison glowered at him and Frank tried to ignore him. The others took scant notice as he mounted and walked to a spot a few yards from where Jesse was ready to ride.

"Just you and me, Slocum. The others will be along presently. I want to have a word with you."

Slocum and the outlaw rode south from Encantado, heading in the direction of Santa Fe. He took a quick look behind and saw Frank James and several others following but making no effort to overtake them. Any hope he had of finishing off Jesse and just riding away was dashed. But then, Slocum still had the hope of learning where Jesse's gold was hidden. While he might turn the outlaw over to Audrey so she could claim a reward—Slocum knew the hell that would raise if he tried turning the outlaw in for the reward himself—there didn't seem a good chance of doing that. What was a paltry few hundred dollars anyway, compared to the hoard Jesse had stashed in some cave in the Sangre de Cristo Mountains? Slocum could certainly do without the infamy of being the one to bring Jesse James to justice. He didn't hanker on spending the rest of his life looking over his shoulder, waiting for somebody to shoot him in the back.

Getting revenge or gaining notoriety as the man who killed the man who had brought in Jesse James didn't matter. Dead was dead.

"You don't seem to be taking to the plan the way the others are, Slocum. There a reason?"

"Occupying Encantado doesn't mean anything to me," Slocum said.

"You want to be part of the bigger plan, don't you? Don't deny it. I knew right away the sort of gent you were. You think big, like me. You have big ambitions."

"Not as big as yours, Jesse, nowhere near as big," Slocum said. That elicited a chuckle from the outlaw.

"You're right as rain about that. I want to be the king of a whole damned country—and I will. I can feel it getting closer by the day."

"Where are we heading?"

"I want you along for a meeting with a merchant from Santa Fe. He's not too inclined toward the current *alcalde* and wants to move up in the world," Jesse said. "Since I figure you're the one to be running Santa Fe for me, it'll be a good thing for you to see what your competition is like."

"Why give me Santa Fe when all you gave Dennison was Encantado?"

"Me and you, Slocum, we have a history. I know what

you can do. You're always thinking. I like that. It keeps me on my toes staying ahead of you, and you're the kind of man I need for a bigger town. When you move up—I can see you as governor of an entire state, as I been telling all the boys—then maybe Charlie will be ready for running Santa Fe."

"You want me to whip it into shape for him," Slocum said, not trying to keep the sarcasm from his voice. If Jesse heard it, he paid no attention.

"That's the kind of thinking I want from you," he said. "You are going to make a fine mayor."

"What do you want from me when you put me in as mayor?"

"See? Dennison would never ask a question like that. He's always thinking only about himself. Well, sir, I want twenty-five percent of all the tax money you rake in. I want you to let me know about train schedules and what's being shipped." Jesse held up his hand to forestall Slocum's comment. "I know, I know, why worry about robbing trains when I have an entire country at my beck and call. You see, the AT&SF will be coming in from Union country."

"You need to be sure the Army's not sending in reinforcements?"

"Reinforcements?" Jesse laughed. "I'll *own* the army in New Mexico Territory. I want to be sure they're not sending in an invasion force."

Slocum rode along as Jesse detailed how he thought the United States would try to retake his country. Slocum had to interrupt him.

"What are you calling it?"

"How's that?"

"Your country. What are you going to call your country?"

Jesse looked perplexed for a moment, then shook his head in wonderment.

"That's another reason I want you sharing the power, Slocum. Dennison would never ask a question like that. Hell, nobody till now has. I've been so busy making my plans, the thought never occurred to me that I'd need a name."

Slocum started to tell him he didn't need to but Jesse halted suddenly and pointed ahead.

"Up there's where we're meeting Stringfellow."

"The merchant?"

"He's in the dry goods business and is worth a fortune. Now hush up and let me do the talking. He's a right skittish fellow." Jesse laughed. "You might call him a skittish String-fellow."

Slocum didn't appreciate the joke all that much but Jesse didn't notice. He was too consumed by his own thoughts of wealth and conquest. A quick look at the back trail showed Frank and two others still followed not a hundred yards away.

"You just watch and see how this goes. You can do the same with other merchants you'll need to bring into the flock." Jesse waved to the merchant.

Slocum saw how nervous Stringfellow looked meeting the notorious outlaw. He dismounted and stood to one side so he could listen to whatever was being discussed.

"Who's that?" Stringfellow said, looking at Slocum.

"Don't worry about him. I need to know you're behind me when this happens."

"You're going to take over the whole town? How?"

"I'll have an army behind me."

"Why do you need me?"

"There'll be people not liking the change in power. What would the town marshal do?"

"He'd fight. He was a sergeant in the Union Army," Stringfellow said. He turned and partially hid himself from Slocum, but Slocum's sharp ears overheard the question. "Is he one of us? A Knight of the Golden Circle?"

Slocum didn't hear Jesse James's answer but it satisfied the merchant.

"Who else in town wouldn't take kindly to someone other than the Federals calling the shots?" Jesse asked.

"There are several prominent merchants," Stringfellow said. Slocum saw the flash of greed on the man's face and knew he was getting ready to condemn business rivals. "You burn them out and the rest would come around fast."

"This is the kind of information I need," Jesse said. "It's the kind of information I pay for." He fumbled in his saddlebags and pulled out a heavy leather bag and tossed it to Stringfellow, who dropped it. When it hit the ground, it spilled out gleaming gold coins.

The merchant pounced on it like a dog on a bone, scooping up the coins and stuffing them into the bag. He looked up at Jesse. Slocum thought he was going to swear allegiance then and there to his new ruler but Stringfellow stood, the bag clutched in both hands.

"I'll let you know if anybody so much as grumbles about it when you take over, Mr. James."

"That's the kind of cooperation I reward," Jesse said. He slapped Stringfellow on the back, put his arm around his shoulder, and steered him away so he could speak confidentially. Slocum made no effort to overhear now. There wasn't anything Jesse could say that could add to everything that had happened.

The two Knights of the Golden Circle spoke, exchanged odd signs and an awkward handshake. Stringfellow left, head bobbing up and down. He climbed into a buggy and drove back toward Santa Fe. Jesse watched him until he was out of sight, then returned to Slocum.

"See how easy it is? All you have to do is drop a few gold coins in front of those pigs and they'll be your oinkers as long as you want."

"Do you really need a spy in Santa Fe?"

"I got more 'n Stringfellow rooting around for me in town," Jesse said. "He's not even the one getting the most money. We're going to have trouble with the law in town. I thought I had a deputy willing to throw in with us, but the marshal caught wind of it and fired him. Ran him out of town. Last I heard, the deputy was down in Albuquerque staying drunk at the White Elephant Saloon and shooting off his mouth about how the marshal was going to pay for running him out of town."

"You afraid he'll alert the cavalry about your plans?"

"Nope." That was all Jesse said, and Slocum knew one of the gang had already been dispatched to permanently close the deputy's mouth.

"What do you intend doing with the list Stringfellow gives you?"

"Might be necessary for you to sneak into town before we stake out claim and remove a few of them. That'll get rid of a passel of problems. We don't want to take too long taking over any one town. We need to grab as many as we can as fast as we can to make it harder for the Army to know where to hit us."

"It could be they'll have to send a telegraph back to Washington asking what to do." Slocum watched Jesse closely. The slight flicker in the man's eyes told him Jesse had already bought the services of the telegraph operators in the places where it would be most beneficial. The mayors or marshals or Army officers might send requests for reinforcements and the telegram would never be sent. Slocum had to hand it to Jesse. The outlaw was acting as if this were a true invasion of a foreign country and took care of what details he could before the actual occupation.

"Where'd the gold come from?" Slocum asked.

"There's more when I need it." Jesse turned brusque. "I got other business. You mosey on into Santa Fe and watch after Stringfellow, see what he does, who he talks to. If he's an honest crook, he'll stay bought."

"But since he could be bought in the first place, he's likely to sell out to anyone offering more," Slocum finished.

"You *do* think on these things real good, Slocum. The

marshal might just trump a bag of gold with threatening to put a bullet in that son of a bitch's head. Never trust a man who can be bought so cheap." Jesse James mounted and rode due east. Over his shoulder he shouted, "Let me know if Stringfellow is inclined to get liquored up and shoot off his mouth. I don't want any of this getting out to the authorities before it's time to move on into town."

Slocum stepped up into the saddle and watched the outlaw join Frank and the others from the gang. All of them rode fast out onto the high desert, in a hurry to get somewhere.

Slocum looked down the road where Stringfellow had gone and considered how he was more interested in finding where Jesse rode than who the merchant talked to in town.

He turned his horse eastward and started after Jesse, traveling slower to keep from being spotted. Jesse—or Frank—would be watching their back trail to be certain no one tracked them.

That made Slocum all the more curious where they went and who they were so eager to meet.

12

Slocum had little difficulty tracking Jesse and the others from his gang. They made no effort to conceal where they rode, making him think Jesse was in a big hurry. He certainly had no reason to think the Army was after him. Slocum wondered how long Berglund would take to get his share of gold. Jesse seemed oblivious to the sergeant's intent to double-cross him whenever he got the payoff.

That made him wonder what Jesse's real game was. The man had carefully thought through the plot to break off this section of New Mexico and claim it for his own. Everything he had done so far had worked, and the number of members in the Knights of the Golden Circle made it possible the scheme might succeed. Stringfellow had been able to exchange secret signs and handshakes. Others in Santa Fe likely were sympathetic, if not in outright alliance with the idea of secession—again.

What happened mattered less to Slocum than raking in some of the gold. That Jesse had it was proved by handing over so much to Stringfellow. If he had given this to Slocum, there'd have been nothing but dust to mark where he'd gone. Slocum had no reason to help the bluecoats keep the civil order anywhere in the territory. If Jesse succeeded in creating a new country, that would only make travel more difficult. Otherwise, it didn't affect Slocum that much.

But the gold. If he could snatch a significant amount of it, a lot of problems would be solved. Jesse wouldn't be able to bribe men like Stringfellow, Berglund would be out the gold and unable to recruit soldiers at Fort Union to join the revolt—and Slocum would be a damned sight richer than he was right now.

Even as he considered how much gold he could make off with, his thoughts wandered to Audrey Underwood. He had no idea where she fit it. The woman seemed like she had no idea what she wanted out of life when she talked of being a reporter and a bounty hunter in the same breath, but something of the treasure hunter lit up her lovely face when she talked about the James Gang's hidden gold. Whatever happened, Slocum had to be cautious around her. She might have told the truth about showing the sheriff a wanted poster on one of Jesse's gang, but it had sounded as if she talked about him.

John Slocum knew there were lawmen all over the West itching to throw him in prison—or worse.

He pulled his bandanna away as sweat caused his neck to itch. That dampness could turn to the scratchy scrape of a hangman's noose if Audrey was lying about what wanted poster she had shown Sheriff Narvaiz.

When he spotted two men on the horizon about a mile ahead, Slocum urged his horse down into an arroyo. He pulled his field glasses from his saddlebags and made his way to the far side of the dry riverbed. Cautious about outlining himself against the horizon as the two riders had, he crept forward, found a rocky rise, and peered over it. A bit of fiddling got the two riders into focus. Both were in Jesse's gang.

From the way they looked away from him, he guessed

they watched something happening not far off. He panned back and forth hunting for some idea what might be going on and then stared hard at a dust cloud rising to the north. It moved slowly toward the spot where he estimated Jesse, Frank, and the handful of others that had ridden with him were gathered.

He jerked about when a cloud of dust rose from the south. Another wagon approached the meeting spot. Or was it? Frowning, he studied the way this dust moved and decided that more than one rider was causing it. He counted no fewer than four separated clouds. Whoever Jesse was meeting not only didn't drive a wagon, but didn't ride in formation either.

Slocum began hiking, watchful that the two sentries might turn and look at their back trail. Ten minutes later, he was within a couple hundred yards and the men had not turned. Their full attention remained on the meeting. More than this, both had their rifles ready and laying across the saddles in front of them.

Finding a ravine that angled in the direction of the wagon, Slocum kept low and worked his way along it until he found a break in the bank that allowed him to look out onto a flat area where the wagon was parked. Zeke sat in the driver's box with Jesse and Frank flanking the wagon. The other two with them were some distance to the east. All of them stared at the approaching riders. From the way Zeke fidgeted, he wasn't comfortable being there, in spite of having six of the meanest outlaws, the deadliest shots, and the most vicious guerrilla fighters to survive the war at his side.

Then Slocum saw the reason for the young outlaw's uneasiness. The riders meeting Jesse were Comanche braves decked out in war paint.

The war chief raised a coup stick and shook it at Jesse, who responded by lifting his rifle and shaking it in the air. This went on for almost a minute, then at some unseen signal both rode forward and met halfway between their respective bodyguards.

Slocum couldn't hear what was being said but the Indian wasn't happy. Jesse raised his voice so Slocum overheard part of the argument.

". . . agreed on the price. You don't get one damned rifle if you don't give us everything we asked."

The Comanche chief argued some more, then pointed his coup stick at Jesse. The feathers dangling from the shaft shook in the hot wind blowing across the plains. Then the Indian grunted and motioned to four of his warriors. They wheeled about and galloped off. Slocum watched them until they were lost in dust from their horses' hooves.

Jesse and the Comanche sat silently, glowering at each other. Slocum swung his field glasses around to see if anyone at the meeting had twigged to being spied upon. All of Jesse's men stared hard at the Indians, who watched only the outlaws. The men might have been chiseled out of marble for all the movement.

After ten minutes Slocum spied another cloud of dust down south. Then the Indians who had left returned with a packhorse struggling under its load.

Jesse hopped to the ground, ignored the Comanche chief's angry outburst, and cut open the canvas over the burden. The chief rode over to the wagon and lifted a tarp with the end of his coup stick. Zeke shifted uneasily, his hand hovering over the butt of his six-gun. Slocum held his breath. If the youngster made a move to throw down on the chief, there'd be blood by the bucket soaking into the sand. Zeke relaxed when the chief let out a whoop and began riding around the wagon, waving his stick in the air.

The Comanche rode to the packhorse, reached down, and cut the rope, freeing the load that thudded to the ground. Slocum caught his breath. He knew where Jesse was getting some of his gold. He was selling rifles to the Indians.

Jesse motioned and his two henchmen came over and

hefted the parcels, staggering with them to the wagon. There, they pulled two cases of rifles out and dropped them to the ground amid a puff of dust. Zeke swung around, pushed another case to them. Ammunition. Two cases of rifles and one of ammunition had changed hands in exchange for however much gold the Indians had paid.

The outlaws got the gold into the back of the wagon. Jesse waved to Zeke, and the young outlaw turned the wagon and headed back in the direction he had come. Jesse waited as the Comanches opened the cases and loaded the rifles, shooting off a few rounds.

Jesse and the chief spoke more amicably, then stepped back and went their separate ways. The rifles and ammunition had been secured to the packhorse, and Zeke was already out of sight with the wagon holding the gold.

Slocum wondered what a couple cases of rifles and the ammo went for. Whatever it was, he would be happy spending it. That it took two men to load into the wagon made Slocum consider ways of getting it away from wherever Zeke took it without using a wagon. He'd have to travel light and fast when he stole it from Jesse James.

"You want us to guard the gold, Jesse?" Frank James rode closer to his brother to talk without shouting. Slocum cursed under his breath when they whispered. Whatever Jesse said made Frank angry. It took several minutes before they parted as amiably as Jesse had from the Comanche war chief. Frank and the other four headed toward Santa Fe but Jesse angled to the northwest, possibly riding for Las Vegas.

Slocum was sure Zeke was driving due north. There weren't any caves in this direction—that he knew of. It surprised him that Jesse trusted a newcomer like Zeke with so much gold. He must think he had the young man wrapped around his little finger with promises of power and authority. The way Zeke had talked about being a governor of an entire state told Slocum a great deal about the youngster. He needed to feel important more than he did rich.

Slocum was sure that Jesse had stressed how a clever man could levy taxes and become rich—but it all flowed from exercise of political power. With the proposed renegade cavalry troopers to back him up, a governor could get by with about anything, as the history of New Mexico under the Spanish had shown.

Slipping away down the ravine, Slocum backtracked to where he had left his horse. He heaved a sigh of relief. He hadn't thought his scouting mission through properly. Frank and the other four men had passed close enough to see the horse tethered in the arroyo. That would have brought them down on his head like an avalanche.

He gripped the saddle horn and pulled himself up, taking one last look around to be sure the outlaws weren't spying on him. A short, low laugh escaped his lips. If Frank James had been anywhere within gunshot, a bullet would have robbed Slocum of his life by now. Frank struck him as far more realistic than his brother when it came to practical matters. Jesse was a dreamer fantasizing about being the ruler of an entire country. Frank was grounded in robbing trains and staying alive.

Slocum rode due north after Zeke. The gold drew him as surely as a compass needle pointed north. Twenty minutes riding brought Slocum to a rockier area well away from the Sangre de Cristos. To his surprise the rocky ground yielded spots that might well hold small caves.

The road Zeke followed hardly took tracks. The ground was sunbaked and hard. When it turned to rock, Slocum had even less trail to follow and relied on the young outlaw not leaving the road. He urged his horse to greater speed, thinking he might change his plan and just steal the wagon, too. He could reach Raton Pass in a day and then consider how best to continue. The wagon team of two horses might be used as pack animals in the higher altitude where breathing became harder. Leave the wagon behind, put the gold on the team, get into Colorado, and disappear.

The longer he rode, the more perplexed Slocum became. It was as if Zeke had simply vanished off the face of the earth.

The hilly terrain hid the road in many places, but when Slocum topped a rise and failed to see the wagon either ahead of him along the road or pulled off anywhere behind, he started to get mad. He wasn't going to be denied the gold!

Slocum pulled his field glasses out and slowly scanned the entire terrain in a full circle. He finally saw what had to be Zeke's trail ahead where he had pulled off the road and headed directly west into the Sangre de Cristo Mountains. The wagon was nowhere to be seen, but the side road provided the only chance for a heavily laden wagon to elude his direct view.

As he lowered the binoculars, a cold knot formed in his belly. Something was wrong. He brought the lenses back to his eyes and saw a horse. Riderless. But the blanket was distinctively patterned with the U.S. Army insignia. As he watched, a soldier came up and mounted. Two more soldiers came into view and then he saw a rider with gold stripes on his arm. Less than a mile behind Zeke rode a squad of cavalry.

No matter who they were, it was bad news for Slocum. If they were some of the soldiers Jesse claimed to have bought off so they would support him when he attacked larger towns, they would guard the gold. And if they were either honest horse soldiers or those riding under Simon Berglund, they'd want to seize the gold. Berglund would keep it, but any other soldier might return to Fort Union with it.

No matter how Slocum cut it, he lost.

He stashed the field glasses in his saddlebags, then rode across country using the hilly countryside to hide his path as he tried to cut off the soldiers and find Zeke and the gold-laden wagon first. He doubted he could convince the young outlaw to split the gold with him and head in different directions, each with his own share. That would confuse any pursuit since Slocum doubted Jesse wanted to divide his forces yet.

And if Zeke didn't want to steal the gold for his own, Slocum could deal with that, too. He hated the idea of shooting it out with Zeke, but he would. The outlaw had been blinded by the lure of power.

Slocum kept his mare moving fast and sure through the hill country, across the road between Las Vegas and Santa Fe, and then toward the mountains. He spotted Zeke struggling to get the wagon up an incline. Just crossing the main road but on the outlaw's trail came the squad of cavalry troopers.

He made a quick decision. Slocum turned away from the wagon and the gold and galloped straight north, kicking up as much fuss as he could. With such a sudden and explosive run, he had to be sighted by the soldiers. And he was. He heard the sergeant's bellowed command and the squad came after him. It was a desperate ploy that kept them from looking in Zeke's wagon and finding the gold.

Slocum considered riding parallel to the road, cutting back and trying to reach Las Vegas. When the soldiers chased him, effectively cutting off that path for him, he turned into the mountains. His mare began to tire, allowing the soldiers to gain on him.

"Stop! Halt!" The sergeant bellowed more, probably curses, but Slocum couldn't hear too clearly since he had found a path between two low hills that cut off all but indistinct echoes.

He looked around constantly as he rode and knew he could never outrace the soldiers. When he saw a Y fork, he galloped up the right branch, then carefully backtracked and took the other route going deeper into the mountains. Slocum jumped from horseback when he heard the sergeant shouting orders, hunkered down, and let his horse rest while he waited and worried about the soldier's skill in tracking. The sergeant stopped at the Y fork, then went to the right.

Only then did Slocum get back into the saddle and ride, hoping he hadn't picked a box canyon. He hadn't. The shallow canyon widened and then fanned out into more level land as he headed back southward. With luck the sergeant would keep his squad riding away long enough for Slocum to entirely disappear. Only he didn't want to disappear, he wanted to find Zeke and take the Comanche gold for his own.

An hour later, he had circled back to the spot where he had last seen Zeke fighting to get his team pulling hard enough to reach a high point in the road. Slocum saw only one place where the wagon could have rolled and headed straight for it. A smile came to his lips when he saw the wagon pulled behind a boulder. The smile died when he realized the team was missing. Riding closer, he saw that the gold in the wagon was also gone.

He jumped to the ground, drew his six-shooter, and went hunting Zeke and the gold.

The dark mouth of a cave opened unexpectedly.

"Zeke?" he called. "You in the cave, Zeke?" When he heard nothing, he advanced cautiously. Slocum expected to see the gold stacked inside, possibly hidden by a pile of rocks. What he found made him mad all over again.

Zeke and the gold were nowhere to be seen, but scratched in chalk on the wall were new symbols. Wherever Zeke had gotten off to with the gold was encrypted in the symbols and numbers.

Slocum didn't have any idea what the ciphers meant.

13

"The wagon's empty. That must mean the gold's in the cave."

The words froze Slocum in his tracks. At least two men were outside near the wagon, and there wasn't anywhere he could run. He looked at the chalk marks on the wall and thought about erasing them, then decided it wouldn't do any good. If those were members of Jesse's gang, they could always ask Zeke to replace the code. And if they weren't, their chance of reading the cipher was as good as his.

None.

Slocum slid his six-gun from his holster and pressed himself against the cold, rocky wall. If he went to the far cave wall, he would run the risk of being pushed back and blunder into the pit. This way he knew he could follow the wall if he had to and miss the pit. A narrow ledge on this side skirted the deep shaft.

"In here, Sarge."

Slocum caught his breath. Berglund and his squad! He raised his pistol and waited for the inevitable. When the face of one of the soldiers he had saved earlier poked around the bend in the cave, Slocum fired. His aim was a little off and the bullet ricocheted against the cave wall, but the effect was just as good as if he had hit the man squarely in the forehead. Rock shards ripped his face and got into his eyes, blinding him.

"He got me, Sarge. Some son of a bitch got me."

Slocum stepped out to the middle of the cave floor and fired twice more. One slug ripped into a soldier's chest and caused him to simply sit down. Slocum knew he was dead. But the other shot missed Sergeant Berglund by inches. He cursed his bad luck and moved forward, ready to fire again. He couldn't let himself be trapped in the cave.

"Fire!"

The command echoed forth an instant before somebody opened up with a rifle. From the muffled report Slocum knew the fourth soldier was firing at him using his carbine. The short rifle barrel caused every shot to be softer, mushier sounding than that from a longer barreled rifle like his Winchester. The thought of his rifle made Slocum wish he had the rifle now. He could blast his way out of this rocky trap.

But he didn't. He got off a couple more shots, hoping to hit Berglund. All he did was send the short, stocky sergeant scampering away to take cover in the rocks near the abandoned wagon.

"My eyes. I'm blind. I can't see nuthin'!" The soldier moaned repeatedly and clawed at his face.

Slocum retreated into the cave and knelt beside the bluecoat. He grabbed his arm and shook until the soldier stopped caterwauling.

"You want to live? You'll do as I say."

"I'm blind!"

"You'll be fine. All you need to do is wash your eyes out with some clean water. But being blind's the least of your worries if you don't do as I say. You're going to be dead otherwise."

"You tried to kill me."

"If I'd meant to shoot you, I would have," Slocum said, lying through his teeth. He *had* meant to kill the soldier and only the darkness in the cave had spoiled his shot. Hastily reloading, Slocum knew he had only seconds before he would never get out of the cave alive. Unless he kept Berglund jumping and guessing, he would never survive a siege.

"I don't want to die," the soldier sobbed out. Slocum knew if the tears kept flowing, the rock dust and shards would eventually wash out on their own. When the man's vision returned, he would be more than a handful. If he didn't coerce his cooperation now, he wasn't going to be able to get it later.

"On your feet," Slocum said, pulling him upright and spinning him around. "You get on out there and tell your sergeant you're all right."

"You're letting me go?"

"Get moving." Slocum shoved him, crouched low, and followed the man as he stumbled forward.

"It's me, Sarge. Don't shoot!"

Slocum knew one of two things would happen. Either Berglund would shoot down his own man or he would be decoyed away from what Slocum intended. It took only an instant to find out what the treasonous sergeant would do. A shot caught the blinded soldier in the middle of the chest.

Slocum caught him up, supporting him with his left arm as he leveled his six-shooter over the collapsing soldier's shoulder. Two quick shots. Berglund and the other soldier fired. Slocum felt the slugs hit the man he held as a human shield. Getting his feet under him, Slocum bent his legs, then heaved, sending the now dead soldier flailing away. The momentary diversion was all he had and he made the most of it.

Feet driving hard, Slocum ran for the cover of a rock a few yards away from the cave mouth. He hit the ground hard, came up, and got off three fast shots that wounded Berglund's surviving partner. The soldier grunted and sat down, clutching his belly. This was all Slocum needed to get off a couple more shots at the sergeant.

"Get back. Retreat, dammit. We have to stop him. Head for higher—"

"Sarge, my gut's on fire. Caught a bullet in the belly."

Slocum might have charged and taken Berglund when the man ripped away the soldier's blouse to expose the wound in his belly. Instead, he wended his way through the rocks and got to his horse. He was out the gold. Wherever Zeke had been told to take it, the lovely metallic coins were probably far out of his reach by now. All Slocum wanted was to get away from Berglund without catching a slug or two.

He swung into the saddle and, riding low, trotted through the winding path until he reached a part of the path that was straight enough to gallop. He expected a few shots to follow him but nothing came. Berglund either was content to tend his wounded man or had gone into the cave, thinking to find the gold. Whether he could decipher the code didn't matter to Slocum now. He rode with the wind and had escaped without catching so much as a sliver of a bullet.

If he stayed on this trail, he would end up back on the road leading to Las Vegas. Zeke had not come this way. If he had, Slocum would have passed him and the two horses laden with the Comanche gold. He swung around to the south and angled back into the foothills. There had to be another path through the rocks, one too narrow for the wagon to traverse.

From the direction of the cave Slocum heard shouting and then a single gunshot. He doubted the private had shot Berglund but the sergeant killing his man because he had botched what ought to have been an easy kill was within the realm of possibility. Whether Berglund tried to hide the bodies or would simply leave them there and explain to Jesse James what had happened didn't bother Slocum unduly.

Jesse could tell when a man was lying—most of the

time. He might need Berglund to worm his way into the underbelly of Fort Union and leave him alive for that reason alone, but the day had to come soon when the outlaw no longer tolerated the double-crossing sergeant. Slocum had seen Jesse get rid of a man or two simply because they displeased him. And those killings had been when Jesse was much younger and less experienced in the ways someone might try to steal his gold.

As if by magic, the trail appeared. Slocum almost missed it in his deep thought about what Berglund was doing and what Jesse would do. A quick glance at the dirt along the rocky path showed recent passage of at least one horse. The hoofprints went in the right direction so Slocum followed. He would overtake Zeke soon enough.

Or so he thought. He spent an hour on the trail before he encountered the young outlaw—riding back toward him.

"Slocum," Zeke said, sadness in his voice. "I didn't believe it would be you."

"What are you talking about?" Slocum was taken unawares when Zeke lifted a shotgun from across the saddle in front of him, leveled it, and fired. The range was too great but one of the 00 buckshot managed to graze Slocum and knock him from the saddle. He landed hard, momentarily stunned.

He heard Zeke riding closer.

"Jesse told me to shoot anybody coming along the trail because he knew they'd be after the gold. I didn't think I'd find anybody, and certainly not you."

"You got it wrong, Zeke. I don't know what you mean about gold." Slocum shook his head but the loud buzzing refused to go away. The fall more than the pellet had discombobulated him.

"He promised me I could be mayor of the city promised to whoever I found. You were gonna be mayor of Santa Fe, weren't you?"

"Take it. I can ride off. Don't . . ." Slocum feinted right

and rolled left in time to avoid another blast from the double-barreled weapon. He went for his six-shooter but froze when he found himself looking down the barrel. It seemed large enough for him to reach his hand into and grab the shell chambered at the far end.

"I thought me and you was good friends, trail companions, Slocum. I was wrong." Zeke lifted the shotgun. Slocum went for his pistol, knowing he could never beat the young outlaw. A shot rang out but something sounded strange about it. Then Zeke slumped forward, twisted to one side, and tumbled from his horse. The animal reared and lashed out with its front hooves, then galloped off in fright.

Slocum sat half propped up, his six-gun still in the holster. He pulled it all the way out when he heard another horse approaching from the direction Zeke had come.

"Are you all right, John?"

"Audrey!" The lovely woman was the last person he expected to see on this trail. She held a rifle, smoke still curling from the muzzle. "You pulled my fat from the fire."

"I don't know what Jesse James told him, but I lost track of the gold. I couldn't follow Jesse because he had a half-dozen men with him, including his brother."

"The gold was lashed to two horses."

"I know. When I couldn't go after them, I decided to see where this one was heading since he'd brought the gold to Jesse."

"A good thing you did." He stared at her. Audrey Underwood didn't seem too perturbed that she had just killed a man. "You going to turn him in for the bounty?"

"Not sure there is one on his head. He just joined up a few days back. He wasn't even dry behind the ears." She shoved her rifle back into the saddle sheath, the stock pointing backward as if she went through heavy brush and wanted to keep the weapon from catching on bushy limbs. There was more about her than he'd thought.

"You really are a bounty hunter, aren't you?"

"And a reporter," she said, smiling. "I might try to write this up for a penny dreadful. Such fiction has become quite popular back East, especially in New York City."

"We might as well head that way," Slocum said. "It's getting mighty dangerous around here." He quickly explained what had happened at the cave after he'd found Zeke's new symbols.

"I can decipher them. He must have placed the location where the gold was being taken into the code. That means someone else is joining Jesse."

"It might mean someone else is joining Jesse, but the cipher doesn't have to reveal the location of the gold anymore. It might give a rendezvous point since Jesse's already got the gold."

"He's probably stashed it somewhere safe by now. I wish I was a better scout. I could have followed and watched." Audrey heaved a deep sigh.

"We might be able to track him together, if you can get me on the right trail."

"You are good at that sort of thing, aren't you, John?"

He grinned and said, "I'm good at all manner of things."

She gave him an appraising look, then wheeled her horse about and set off at a brisk walk. He shook the cobwebs from his head, then mounted. It didn't surprise him that he was a little woozy. The pellet had grazed his skull and shaken him up. He urged his mare to greater speed to catch up with Audrey, then he slowed. From behind he got a good view of the her riding form—and her own womanly form. When she half turned to look back to see if he was keeping up, he got a silhouette view of her that set his heart to beating just a little faster. The gentle bobbing up and down made her into a vision of pure sexiness.

"There," she said, coming to a halt. "This is the trail they took over the hills."

"Due west is Taos. To the southwest is Encantado. That's where I'd bet he's headed."

"Why'd Jesse want to go to a nothing of a town like Encantado?"

Slocum explained how the gang had ridden down on the town and seized it as the first of what the outlaw expected to be a series of rapid conquests.

"This is amazing," Audrey said. "You told me what the gang intended doing, but somehow I discounted it as being too completely outrageous. Jesse James is actually going to establish a country for the Knights of the Golden Circle."

"He's going to try. It'll take more than one sleepy, dusty town and a small mountain of gold to bring the entire territory under his sway."

"The journey of a thousand miles begins with a single step."

Slocum just stared at her, wondering what she meant. But he pulled his eyes off her to the Sangre de Cristos rising a few miles beyond. They had ridden through the foothills, but the mountains themselves were rugged, ragged, and difficult to cross. Unless you were a thunderstorm.

"Lightning," Slocum said. He had seen the flash and the thunder came a few seconds later, spooking his horse. "That storm's boiling up over the mountains and coming right at us."

"There's no point going after Jesse James in a rainstorm," she said. "We'd better hole up somewhere."

"I saw a likely spot a quarter mile back along the trail."

"The cave?"

Audrey continued to surprise him.

"I wanted to be sure we weren't riding past a couple of the gang waiting to ambush us. That would have been a great spot."

"I know. I thought the same thing. But nobody'd disturbed the dirt in front of the cave, except for some small animals. I didn't see any bear tracks."

Again she surprised him with her observation. All he had wanted to be sure of was the lack of men with rifles trained on them as they rode past. They returned to the cave and a quick look at the terrain around the cave confirmed what Audrey had said. Coyotes and maybe a wolf had entered the cave—and left—but nothing bigger. No sign of a puma or bear.

Slocum jumped to the ground as the first watery fist struck at his face. He pulled down his hat to protect himself, then tugged hard to lead his horse into the cave. The entrance was small but immediately inside widened enough for two horses to be stabled for the night.

"It's good if we sleep between them and the weather," Audrey said. "The storm's getting downright bad."

"You're almost soaked," Slocum said. She had followed him in. The brief added time she was outside had seen her drenched by the downpour. He liked the look of her blouse stuck against her skin. He could see every delightful contour and imagine even the moles and freckles.

"What are you staring at, mister?" she said with mock severity. "You never seen a woman this wet before?"

"Not recently."

"Then I'd better get out of these clothes and dry them. If I had a fire, that is."

Slocum hobbled their horses at the back of the cave, then hurried out to gather what dried wood he could find. By the time he had returned, he was soaked to the skin, too.

He stopped just inside the mouth of the cave and stared. Audrey had shed all her clothing and sat with the blanket wrapped around her. Or rather, the blanket was almost wrapped around her. Enough bare skin showed to give him a tantalizing view of her breasts, her legs, and even a hint as she moved of the tangled thatch between those shapely thighs.

"Don't just stand there," she said. "Start a fire. I want to warm up."

"Right away," he said. As he worked, he found it increasingly difficult to concentrate because Audrey had dropped the blanket and moved behind him, working off his gun belt and coat, vest and shirt, then starting on his jeans. As the last button of his fly popped open, she caught at the fleshy handle that stuck up from his groin.

He gasped when she began moving it up and down like a pump.

"Hard to get the fire started with you doing that," he grated out.

"Yes, it *is* hard," she agreed, putting her cheek against his bare back but never relinquishing her hold on him. Her hand moved up and down slowly, giving him lightning flashes to match those outside. The rain hammered down but they were safe in the cave. When he finally ignited the wood, they had a chance to be dry also.

But by this time neither of them paid a whole lot of attention to laying out their clothes so they'd dry faster. They were locked in each other's arms, kissing passionately and moving with increasing need, their bodies sliding back and forth. Slocum wanted everything but he found himself with a woman whose damp skin made it hard to hang on. Audrey slipped and slid until she was in the position she wanted.

On hands and knees, she looked over her shoulder at him.

"Go on," she urged. "I'm feeling lusty, like an animal. Take me like an animal. I—" He cut her off by moving behind, giving her rounded butt a quick slap and then moving forward even more. He gripped the fleshy half-moons of her ass and parted them slightly to give himself a direct shot inward. His hips levered forward, the bulbous tip of his manhood rubbed along her moist nether lips, and then he sank into her heated center.

It was his turn to be speechless. The sensations flooding his body robbed him of all rational thought. All he knew burned at his groin, in his loins. He gripped her waist and pulled her backward. Her ass fit the curve of his body perfectly and they remained unmoving for what seemed forever. She surrounded his length totally with warmth and increasing wetness as her desires mounted.

Then Slocum could remain still no longer. He pulled back, then surged forward at the same time he pulled on her waist. She got into the rhythm and soon all he needed to do was balance himself. She was thrusting her hips back as he moved forward so they collided with growing power. He sank deeper into her with each thrust until the power began to take its toll on him. His control slipped away.

She reached down through their legs and began fondling his dangling sac, which tightened even more at her touch. With her cheek resting on the blanket, she let out one long, low moan after another.

"Hurry, John. I . . . I can't stand more. Faster, go faster."

He obliged. He felt the friction burning at him, at her, consuming them both. When he reached the point of no return, a thunderclap outside marked their mutual release. Another eye-dazzling bolt followed and then even Audrey's moans of pleasure were drowned out by the crashing of rain against the rocks.

Spent, Slocum slipped forward. His arms wrapped around her and held her close. She shivered now so he pulled the blanket around them.

"This is so nice, John, so nice." She began to drift off, but just before she fell sound asleep, Slocum heard her mutter, "Gold, so much gold."

Then he let the sounds of the storm lull him to sleep, too, with visions of gold shooting through his dreams.

14

Slocum stirred and reached out. Audrey wasn't beside him. He sat up and reached for his six-shooter, but there wasn't any cause. She was hunkered down beside the fire. When Slocum had lit it, the fire was low with only a few twigs to fuel it. Audrey had found enough wood to stoke it up and dry her clothing.

"There," she said, not turning. She had sensed he was awake. "Your clothes are washed and dried."

"Washed?"

"From walking through the rain," she said. Audrey turned, brushed back tangled hair from her eyes, and said, "So how do we find the gold?"

Slocum laughed. She was as single-minded about the shiny gold metal as he was.

"Jesse was on his way to Encantado," he said. "He wouldn't stash the gold in town, though. He told Zeke to put the symbols in the other cave to tell somebody else where the gold would be kept."

"So Zeke didn't know what the cipher meant?" Audrey

nodded slowly as she thought on this. "But Jesse's not riding around New Mexico with the gold."

"This was a small amount of what he likely has. The real question is who is he giving directions to? Who's going to decipher the code on that cave wall and find their way to the gold?"

"He's recruiting men steadily now. I got a telegram from my editor in Kansas City saying some of Jesse's cousins are on the way here. Or at least they've left Missouri and are riding west. Where else would they be going?"

"So he's making sure his family knows where the gold is." Slocum dressed slowly, aware of Audrey watching him closely. He strapped down his gun belt before he said anything more. "Is this like a last will and testament—his legacy?"

"He's a shrewd man," Audrey said. "He might want Frank or one of his cousins to continue the revolt if he's killed."

"Jesse thinks he'll live forever," Slocum said. It was possible that Jesse James had changed over the years since he had ridden with him, but Slocum doubted it. The gold was intended to pay off soldiers like Berglund and others throughout the territory. Jesse might give them the key to decipher the code so they could retrieve the gold and perform their duties to the Knights of the Golden Circle. He might even be leaving the precious metal for gunrunners as middlemen in the illicit trade of selling rifles to the Indians.

There wasn't a whole lot Slocum didn't think Jesse James was capable of doing, as long as it was illegal.

"We ought to try to find the gold." Audrey's tone was almost plaintive.

Slocum started to ask her about the stack of wanted posters she had shown to Sheriff Narvaiz, then reconsidered. He didn't want to know the answer. She might have shot Zeke to protect her investment in Slocum. Zeke was a newcomer to the outlaw trail and didn't have a price on his head. For all Slocum knew, the wanted poster Audrey had only paid for John Slocum being delivered alive and kicking—so he could kick his last at the end of a rope.

"Why are you looking at me so strangely, John?"

"Never seen such a lovely bounty hunter," he said.

"You mean treasure hunter. I fully intend to recover the gold the James Gang has stolen."

"And turn it in for a reward?" He read the answer in the shock on her face. "I didn't think so."

"I can be many things to many men, can't I?" Audrey flounced around, kicking at the fire and looking out into the bright, clear spring day. "My editor ought to be waiting for a new story from me anytime now."

"What do you get paid for your reporting?"

"Not nearly enough. That's why I have my eye on the stolen gold."

"You'd steal what's already been stolen?" The thought amused Slocum because that was the way he considered the gold. It didn't rightly belong to Jesse because he had stolen it, so stealing from a thief made it all right to keep the gold for himself.

"You make it sound . . . wrong."

"Do you think you could decode the cipher in the cave?"

"I was on my way there when I came across you at the wrong end of a shotgun. If I can decipher the location, I— we—can wait for Jesse to leave it unguarded and then take it for ourselves."

Slocum only nodded. Jesse wouldn't post a guard on it. Why go to the trouble of hiding it if you kept sentries looking over it? What Slocum worried about more was Audrey claiming she wasn't able to figure out the message, then going to retrieve the gold herself.

"Well, let's ride. I'm anxious to become quite rich."

Slocum kicked out the fire, took the hobbles off the

horses, and led them outside into the bright morning sunlight. The day was about perfect for riding and it took them almost no time to return to the cave where the encrypted message had been left. Slocum noted how Audrey made a point of lifting her chin and pretending not to see what the coyotes had done to Zeke as they rode past the outlaw's body. In another day there wouldn't be any flesh remaining on his bones. In a month, even the bones would be scattered and Zeke would be returned to the earth.

It was more fitting a burial than he deserved. Slocum still pictured the huge bores of the shotgun pointed at him. He touched the scab forming on the side of his head where the single pellet had almost killed him. Zeke's ambition had far outstripped his friendship.

"The wagon!" Audrey said, excited. "It's—"

"Abandoned," Slocum told her. He dismounted and looked around. The heavy rain had scrubbed the ground clean. No one had entered the cave since the rain had stopped sometime around dawn.

"We should be careful about leaving our footprints," Audrey said. "Is there any way we can get in and out without signaling that we've been here?"

"We can walk along the rocks almost to the cave mouth. If you jump, you can miss the dirt right in front of the cave and then inside there's nothing but rocky floor."

"Well, all right," Audrey said, dubious of the scheme. She watched Slocum traverse the rocks, then gather his legs under him and launch through the air. He missed the rocky part by inches and left a deep heel print in the mud.

"Wait a minute," he said, kneeling and using a flat rock to move mud around and smooth over the depression he'd made. It took only a few seconds but if they had tromped into the cave and then out, even stepping in their own tracks as they retreated, it would have been the work of an hour to erase the prints. Even worse, the effort would be obvious to anyone noticing how the mud had formed in ridges and ripples from the wind. The careful work he did on the heel print would be apparent, too, if someone looked but they'd have to go over the ground far more carefully to find his handiwork.

"Are you ready, John?" Audrey stood on the same rock and chewed her lower lip as she concentrated on the jump. "Here I come!"

She arced through the air but would have come down short of the rocky cave floor where Slocum stood if he hadn't reached out, caught her around her trim waist, and swung her about to lightly set her down.

"That was quite the experience," she said, trying to pat her hair into place and failing. She smoothed her skirt and then went directly to the message written on the wall.

Slocum saw how water had seeped into the cave and tiny rivulets had blurred part of the coded message. He stood back, lit a lucifer, and looked at the entire wall, trying to decipher what Zeke had written. He finally gave up. Audrey muttered to herself, ran her fingers over some of the more indistinct symbols, and finally turned to him, a smile on her lips.

"I've figured it out. Many of the symbols are common to other Knights of the Golden Circle caches. The only spot where I had to work at all hard to figure it out was here." She tapped the spot were many of the symbols were smudged from the rainwater dripping over them. "This gives the location."

"Back the way we came?"

"On the other side of the pass and, if I'm right, about five miles north of Encantado."

"I was right about Jesse not keeping the gold with him. He's not the kind to spend the night on the trail in a downpour. He'd want a roof over his head and a bottle of tequila in his hand."

"There's something you're not telling me, John. I can sense it. Why don't you trust me?"

"We might get ourselves shot up at any instant. Jesse's gang is on the move everywhere in these parts."

"So you're worried about my safety? How sweet." Audrey went to him and gave him a kiss on the cheek. "You don't have to. After all, I saved your life."

Slocum wasn't sure what she was saving it for. She might need him to fight off Jesse's gunmen so she could get to the gold, or she might be saving him for the sheriff. He couldn't discount the possibility that Audrey planned both. Find the gold, then turn him in to the sheriff so she could both collect the reward on his head and take the gold for herself.

"We know the trail," he said. "The hardest part will be leaving the cave so nobody'll know we were here." And he was right. Scrambling up the rocks left signs he couldn't hope to erase, but they were in such places that only someone looking for them would notice.

The ride back across the hills went fast, but Slocum had miscalculated how long it would be for Zeke's bones to vanish. As they rode past the spot where the outlaw had died, no trace remained. Some larger predator had dragged off the body. Ashes to ashes, dust to dust . . .

By late afternoon they approached a low hill that seemed to just pop out of the ground. It was covered with lush grass and more than a few trees, mostly piñon and juniper. It didn't look like the sort of place where a cave might just open up, and it wasn't.

"Buried," Audrey said in disgust. "That must be what they've done with it. But it'll be easier to find since the turned dirt will be fresh."

"Not that easy after last night's rain," Slocum pointed out. "But they might not have buried it in the way you think." He pointed to a dilapidated windmill.

"That's about the right spot for the gold," Audrey said. "But why would Jesse leave anything at such an obvious spot?"

Slocum dismounted and let his horse work on eating as much of the juicy grass as possible while he went to the windmill. He looked up and saw that several rungs nailed to one leg were broken off.

"Up there?" Audrey followed his gaze skyward. "That seems crazy, but the rungs were broken off recently. See how the exposed wood on the leg isn't as weathered as spots above and below?"

Slocum tested the structure. It was rickety but strong enough to hold his weight. Working his way up the wooden leg, taking advantage of the strongest rungs and avoiding putting his weight on those likely to give way, he finally reached the splintery platform next to the windmill blades. The gears were broken and the assembly wouldn't turn to track the wind, but he saw how the long shaft down to the well was bent.

"Is it there?" Audrey called up.

Slocum looked at the broken boards and saw no place for gold to be hidden, yet someone had crawled up here recently. He stood and looked around. From here he could see the outskirts of Encantado. Maybe Jesse had sent one of his men up here to act as lookout while the gold was hidden elsewhere. Hanging on to the blades, Slocum looked down to where Audrey shielded her eyes to peer up at him.

"Nothing, John? Nothing at all?" She sounded vexed.

Slocum lowered his gaze from the horizon to the area around the base of the windmill, near the spot where the shaft had gone into the ground to pump up water from the well below.

"To your left," he called down. "There are rocks that've been moved recently. "More. Go farther. There!"

He watched as Audrey hastily began moving the rocks he had spotted. The dirt around the stones had been cut up not too long back. From ground level it wasn't as obvious, but from up here he saw the difference in color of the soil immediately. Leaning farther out, he saw Audrey take the final rock from the cairn. Her shoulders slumped as she sat back on her heels.

She looked up and shouted, "Empty. Nothing here."

Slocum worked his way down the leg and dropped the final few feet. He pulled a few splinters from his callused hands as he went to the hole in the ground where Audrey had returned to paw around in the mud at the bottom. She found something and held it up.

Gold glinted through a coat of mud.

"One coin. One coin!" He thought she was going to cry in frustration.

"That means more had been hidden here but were taken out."

"So fast? There wasn't time for anyone to see what Zeke had scrawled. We would have seen evidence! We would have passed them."

"Might be that's only one place telling where to find the gold. Jesse might be advertising this particular place all over."

"Could be," Audrey said morosely, turning the coin over and over in her hand. She wiped off the mud and stared at the shining coin. "You want it?"

"Pay for your boardinghouse," Slocum said.

"What do we do now?"

"Things are likely to move pretty quick," Slocum said. "If we wait, we'll be in the middle of it." He was afraid he was all too right about that. Jesse knew that he had to move fast once he began his rebellion. The longer he waited, the sooner the Army would send troops in from the rest of the country to crush his uprising. The more territory he controlled, the less likely the U.S. government was to try to pry him loose. If he commanded a significant number of troopers from Fort Union, that made his seizure of New Mexico Territory all the more dangerous.

"I'm not the kind to sit and watch," Audrey said. "I ought to go after Jesse."

"You'll end up dead," Slocum told her. "He's got a body-guard around him all the time. I doubt Frank leaves his side, and tangling with Charlie Dennison is a damned sight more dangerous than dealing with a tenderfoot like Zeke."

"Zeke had you dead to rights."

"Dennison is worse," Slocum said harshly.

"Oh, all right. I'll go back to Las Vegas. Will you be there anytime soon?"

Slocum considered what he could do and finally said, "A few hours after you. If I can find Jesse, I'll settle scores with him."

"That won't stop the rebellion."

"I know, but a snake without a head isn't quite as dangerous. Frank James is a clever outlaw but he's not as devious as Jesse—he doesn't have the skill getting men to follow him on crazy missions like this."

"You don't get yourself killed, John." She kissed him quickly, then mounted and headed back over the pass through the hills on her way to Las Vegas.

Slocum watched her go, worrying that she might run into some of the gang. Then he decided whatever was going on right now would command all of Jesse's attention. If Jesse was involved, the rest of his gang was, too. He poked about in the hole hunting for more dropped coins but found nothing. Replacing the stones over the hole gave him time to think. When he'd finished, he knew what he had to do and where to go.

He rode south to Encantado, entering the town like his head was on a spring. He tried to look everywhere at the same time, worrying about snipers shooting him out of the saddle. The cantina Jesse had used as a headquarters looked empty. For all that, the entire town was eerily quiet. He dismounted and poked his head inside. Cigar smoke and stale beer made his mouth water. He needed a drink and he needed a smoke, but he called out to the barkeep seated at the back of the long, narrow room.

"Where's Jesse and the rest?"

"Dunno. Gone. They drunk up all my best whiskey, then they rode out a couple hours ago."

"Where'd they go?" Slocum saw no amount of questioning was going to pry the answer from the bartender. It might well be that he didn't know since Jesse had no reason to share such information with a man who did nothing more than pour liquor and draw warm beer.

He went outside and caught sight of a couple people sneaking a look at him from behind curtains. Slocum swung into the saddle and rode south another mile before he found the road curving up from Santa Fe. Here he looked in the direction of that town and then twisted around and tried to make out the tracks in the road. The rain had done too good a job of wiping away any old tracks and the new were indistinct.

Having to choose between Santa Fe and Las Vegas, he decided upon Las Vegas, wondering if Audrey being there had anything to do with his decision. He hoped not. She was still a burr under his saddle and would be until he figured out if she was intent on turning him in to Sheriff Narvaiz for any reward on his head.

He rode slowly, letting his horse pick its way past mud puddles and deeper potholes in the road. After a couple miles he urged his horse to greater speed because he saw more evidence that a large number of riders had passed this way recently. Jesse was making his bid. Slocum knew it.

When he came within a half mile of the outskirts of Las Vegas, he heard gunfire. He galloped forward and saw buildings on fire. Then came a curtain of gunshots that took him back to the war and all-out battles.

Jesse James had launched his war to create a breakaway country.

15

Slocum rode into the tumult, aware that he was a sitting duck in the middle of the street. More than one bullet tore past him, but none came as close as the buckshot pellet that Zeke had fired his way. Smoke from burning buildings toward the plaza made his nose wrinkle and eyes water. He pulled up his bandanna, then worried this might make him more of a target from the townspeople as they rushed out. He didn't want to look like an outlaw, even if Jesse James thought he was riding with his gang.

More shots echoed from ahead as Slocum caught sight of Charlie Dennison riding at a full gallop, firing left and right until his six-shooter came up empty. Like Quantrill's Raiders had done years before during the war, he shoved the empty pistol into his belt, drew a second six-gun, emptied it, and repeated with yet a third pistol. In only a few seconds, Dennison had unleashed eighteen shots. Then he turned down a crossing street and disappeared from sight. Slocum followed the reports from a fourth six-shooter and then any more shooting from the outlaw was drowned out from three others charging toward him.

"Slocum!"

He lifted his six-shooter but held his fire. He could shoot Jesse James from the saddle, but the men with him would cut him down before he could get off a second shot. The wild expressions and way they sweat told of their excitement— their fanaticism. They were in a killing frenzy and wouldn't slow down until they ran out of ammunition.

"You started the revolt," Slocum called. "Why did you do it now?"

"Time was right. We hold Encantado, so we had to keep moving on. Glad you could make it. Where have you been?"

"Somebody killed Zeke," Slocum said, thinking this might explain his absence since he didn't want to tell Jesse he had been looking to steal his gold.

"Damnation, I wondered if that boy had run off. He didn't seem the type I need for work like this."

Work. That word burned through Slocum's brain. That was all Jesse James thought of shooting up Las Vegas. The deaths, the destruction, none of that mattered because it was only a way toward prying loose the territory. If he wasn't stopped, he would cause even more misery.

"What're your plans?" Slocum asked.

"We're driving back the peons with rifles and burning their houses. If they give up, they're safe from us."

Putting this to the lie, one outlaw with Jesse turned and fired several times into the chest of a man coming from an adobe house with his hands above his head. Jesse paid no heed.

"You have enough men to occupy the town?"

"More every hour, but we got problems right now."

"Jesse," Frank James called. "They got themselves a cannon."

The words were hardly out of the man's mouth when the familiar roar of cannonade rumbled down the street and almost knocked Slocum from the saddle. He clung to the saddle horn as his horse staggered. He was partially deafened but heard the cries of fear and shrieks from small children and women as they fled.

"We got—"

Frank James's words were drowned out by a second shot. This time Slocum had turned his back to the blast, and it only sent his horse scuttling along a few paces.

"We gotta take them out or we're gonna get pushed back," Frank concluded.

"Come on, Slocum. I remember you were good at frontal assault." Jesse wheeled about, waited to see if Slocum was joining him, then tore back down the street toward the plaza. Riding full tilt into the mouth of a cannon was crazy, but so was Jesse James. Slocum followed, aware that Jesse's flanking gunmen were right behind him, with a half-dozen pistols crammed into their belts and bandoliers. Their firepower exceeded his own. Even if he managed to shoot one out of the saddle, the other would take him. As they rode, Slocum waited for a stray shot to kill one or the other of the outlaws behind him. That would make his own response easy—just one to shoot.

Lady Luck betrayed him. Through the smoke and death they rode unscathed.

"There they are," Jesse said, pointing with one of his pistols at a small knot of men struggling to load and turn the cannon against the outlaws. "You think we're up for it? Remember how we hit them bluecoats along the Centralia road? We swarmed 'em before they knew we were there."

"This gun crew knows where we are," Slocum said. He put his heels to his horse to duck down a side street as he saw the man with the lanyard put a hand over the ear closest to the cannon and yank hard with the other.

The blast knocked Slocum's mare to its knees. He urged the horse to get back up and looked behind him, hoping the shot had removed some of his woe. The angle had been wrong and the shot had gone high, above the gang's heads and into a two-story building that once had been a hotel.

Now it was nothing more than blown-apart wood frame that fitfully burned here and there where the cannonball had ripped through.

"Come on, Slocum, we got them now!"

Jesse and the others charged, firing as they went. Slocum followed more slowly but still saw how the outlaws gunned down the three-man crew on the cannon.

"We got the cannon now and can use it ourselves. We can control the plaza."

Slocum took a shot at Charlie Dennison but the man ducked. Slocum saw that the missed shot struck a man trying to lift a long-barreled goose gun. Dennison looked from the man writhing in the street to Slocum and back. Dennison made quick work of the fallen man. Slocum lifted his Colt again to take out Dennison but the hammer fell on an empty chamber. He fired twice more. Both empty. Unlike the gang, he had only the one six-shooter. He cursed the soldier who had stolen his other six-gun. That would have doubled his firepower and allowed him to take Charlie Dennison out of the saddle.

He reloaded, but by the time he was ready to fire again, Dennison was nowhere to be seen.

Jesse and Frank were on the far side of the plaza driving back a small crowd armed with nothing more than ax handles and hammers.

Slocum's mare reared and turned about, letting him look back down the street at stolidly marching soldiers, four abreast and at least a dozen in rank behind the leading men. They had their rifles lowered and bayonets fixed. He waved to them. Then his heart sank when he saw Sergeant Berglund on a horse trailing them, barking orders and forcing them to press on to the center of town.

"Jesse, we got company. Hell, we got a whole company!" Charlie Dennison had appeared from a side street. He laughed uproariously and Slocum knew these soldiers were ones bought and paid for using the hidden gold. If

Berglund had given up trying to steal the gold from the outlaws, he might have decided he could profit by throwing in with them.

Whatever Berglund's reasons, he kept his men marching at a quick step until they spilled into the plaza. Half went in one direction and rest marched counter until they had the few fighters surviving in the plaza surrounded.

"Go on, General," Jesse bellowed. "Have at 'em!"

"Fire!" Berglund's command was instantly obeyed. Forty rifles fired and the half-dozen trapped citizens died. "Advance and use bayonet."

The soldiers exchanged looks now, as if they hadn't expected this. Then they began closing the ring and moving to the plaza center. One or two made stabbing motions but most of the soldiers passed by the bodies. Either they spared the lives of the wounded—or there weren't any wounded to spare.

"We got ourselves a town, a big one now," Jesse chortled. "See, Slocum, see what a little gold'll do?"

Slocum fell back rather than let Berglund see him. For all he knew, the sergeant thought he was dead and buried out on the high desert. He tried to pick out any of the four soldiers he had saved what seemed an eternity ago but couldn't find any of them. They were the ones most likely to recognize and betray him.

"This way, Slocum," Jesse yelled. "We got ourselves a powerful lot of town to subdue."

"It's different occupying it rather than just shooting it up," Slocum called to the outlaw. Jesse only laughed and started firing through windows as he rode. There wasn't going to be a pane of glass intact within a mile of Las Vegas after the James Gang finished this day.

Slocum fell farther back and was glad because someone had organized a few men with rifles. They lined both sides of the street and caught Jesse and his bodyguards in a blistering cross fire. Two of the gunmen at Jesse's side collapsed and fell to the ground, but Jesse was leading a blessed life today. In spite of the hail of bullets, he rode past unscathed.

Slocum saw the marshal step out and knew where the organizing had bubbled up from. The lawman began shooting methodically at Jesse. Again the outlaw's luck held. Not a bullet even made him flinch.

"So you're the one responsible for this?" Jesse motioned. A half-dozen men appeared from down the street to back his play. "Burn the buildings to the ground."

"You son of a bitch. You won't get by with this!" The marshal fired until his six-shooter came up empty. He began reloading, then turned, and looked over his shoulder. "You'll pay now, you no-account snake! That's the Army come from Fort Union to rescue us."

Slocum didn't see who shot the marshal. It might have been Jesse or any of his men. More likely it was a soldier in the front rank marching down the street.

"Burn 'em out. You bluecoats know how to do that. You did it enough times during the war," Jesse called. He laughed, then continued down the street, firing as he went.

"Don't," Slocum said, riding to the corporal dispatching a half-dozen men to carry out Jesse's orders. "He was just shooting off his mouth. He wants you to secure the plaza. There's another attack planned there."

"Who the hell are you?"

"I'm Jesse's right-hand man," Slocum said. When the corporal wasn't buying that, he added, "Right after Frank, of course. He's family." This caused a small seed of doubt to grow. Slocum might have sent the soldiers on their way back to the plaza but some brave soul in the building in front of them thrust a rifle through a broken window pane and started firing. One soldier went to his knees, clutching his leg. The rest swung around like the well-drilled military unit they were and fired until the clapboard wall turned to dust and the roof sagged down far enough to eventually collapse on anyone inside.

"Don't pay no nevermind to him. Do as Mr. James ordered. Burn 'em out!"

Slocum raised his pistol and shot the corporal. That produced a moment where the world froze around them. The soldiers didn't know what to do, and those still willing to fight hiding inside the buildings were similarly confused. They had an ally that rode with Jesse James and called him by name, yet was trying to save them.

The muzzle blast of the cannon in the town square broke the spell. Two soldiers swung their Spencer rifles around and opened fire on him. Slocum had no choice but to beat a hasty retreat, trying not to get his hide filled with Union lead. Somehow, this time was no better than when he had fought in the war. He ducked low, kept his mare running, and finally turned a corner into a quiet street where heavy black smoke hung like a choking fog. The only salvation here was the lack of bullets flying toward him.

"Help me, please." The woman's plaintive cry was too much for Slocum to ignore. He dismounted and made his way past a mountain of dead horses and saw a woman kneeling down, a man's head in her lap. She looked up at him, eyes filled with tears. "He's hurt. I don't know how to help him."

Pink froth boiled from the man's mouth, warning Slocum that a bullet had pierced a lung and caused air to rush in through the wound. He ripped open the man's shirt and saw he was right. Not much blood marked the entry wound and after rolling the man onto his side, he didn't see any exit wound. That would be bad, having the slug stay inside, but there'd be no time for a doctor to operate if the sucking chest wound wasn't fixed in a hurry.

Slocum rolled the man over.

"Keep his head in your lap so he doesn't drown in his own blood." This set the woman to sobbing hysterically. "You listen up or he'll die in your arms." Slocum fished through his pockets and found a silver dollar. He hated to part with it, but a man's life hung in the balance. Slocum wasn't sure it was worth a dollar but quieting the woman would be. He pressed the coin down hard over the bullet wound.

The man gasped, spewed out more pink froth, and began breathing more normally.

"He's hurt bad but if you keep the coin pressed into his side as hard as you can, he won't die right away. He needs a doctor pronto."

"D-Down the street. Go fetch him. H-He's the only one in town."

"He's not going to come out here to operate," Slocum said, looking around. He saw an overturned cart, righted it, and heaved the man into it. "Keep the coin pressed in tight. Don't worry about bruising him. He's got more to worry about than sore ribs." The woman sniffled but was getting herself under control. "He your husband?"

She nodded. That was as good as Slocum wanted from her. He grabbed his horse's reins and lashed them to the cart, then lifted the handles and began pushing. The man in the cart groaned and his eyelids fluttered open. Slocum doubted he saw much, but the woman took it as a sign that he was going to survive.

About when Slocum's back was starting to hurt from bending over to shove the cart along, he saw the doctor's sign. He dropped the cart outside the door and told the woman, "I've got to go. Get the doctor. I'll keep your husband breathing until you get the sawbones."

The man's eyes opened again and he rasped out, "Thanks."

Then the doctor came out and began barking orders. He went back into his office and returned with tape and a heavy bandage, which he shoved down on the wound. Slocum took his bloody silver dollar back.

He stepped away, then he mounted and rode while the doctor and woman wrestled to get the wounded man inside. Slocum didn't hold out much hope. He had seen too many wounds like that during the war. The lucky ones were shot so that the bullet went clean through them. The doctor was likely to kill his patient trying to get the slug out, but Slocum had other fish to fry. Staying alive was high on his list of things to do.

Seeing the woman had sparked his memory of telling Audrey to return to town and wait for him. The only place he knew where she might be was at the boardinghouse. The edge of town was likely to be safer than anywhere else, but Slocum wanted to get her out of danger. He made his way through the burning town. Gunshots were more sporadic now, telling him that Jesse had won the battle and now cleaned up small pockets of resistance. With the company of soldiers at his back, he could hold control, regroup his gang, and then move on to their next conquest.

With the merchant from Santa Fe likely working to subvert authority in that town, Slocum knew the next town to fall. If Fort Union was under his control, Jesse had only a few small towns to subdue. Raton might be next since he could control access through the mountain pass. Slocum shook his head as he rode, marveling that an outlaw like Jesse James was succeeding so quickly and easily.

Dozens were dead and half of Las Vegas was in flames, but adobe didn't burn and roofs could be replaced easily enough. The wood and frame buildings would be destroyed but along the main street were enough businesses constructed using brick that most would remain after the shooting died down.

The Knights of the Golden Circle might actually succeed. Slocum was glad there hadn't been anyone to take his bet against that happening. Eventually Washington would bring enough might against the breakaway territory to draw it back into the fold, but by then Jesse's dream of Mexico, Central America, and some of the Caribbean islands joining his new slave-holding country might make that retaking extremely expensive.

The president might not want to risk a second war and

let Jesse and those in cahoots with him keep their own country. For all he knew, there might be senators who would argue this in exchange for a governorship or other juicy political plum position offered by the Knights of the Golden Circle.

Slocum finally got past the worst of the smoke and coughed a few times to clear his lungs. He rode straight for the boardinghouse but caught his breath when he saw several horses outside. The front door stood open and a commotion came from inside.

A single shot sent Slocum galloping forward but good sense finally prevailed. He couldn't take on four of Jesse's gang. One horse he recognized as belonging to Charlie Dennison. He would fight Dennison anywhere and anytime using any weapon, but right now wasn't likely to give him any chance of winning. Dennison would have his henchmen join in the fight. Slocum could take him. He knew that. But not Dennison and three others.

Riding around to the rear of the house, Slocum hit the ground and ran to a window. He peered into the kitchen and saw Señora Gonzales sprawled on the floor. He knew where the single shot had been directed. A huge red splotch on her breast showed someone's accuracy. She had been shot straight through the heart.

Slocum opened the kitchen door and slipped inside. He stepped over the dead woman, being careful not to slip in her blood.

"This the one, Charlie?"

"She's the one. Bring her along."

Audrey's voice cut through him like a knife.

"You won't get away with this. My friend'll stop you. He'll *kill* you!"

"Yeah, your friend," Dennison sneered. "I might just save you as bait to lure him into a trap."

"He's too smart for that!"

Dennison's cold laugh was all the answer Audrey got. Slocum heard scuffling and then silence.

He spun around, six-shooter leveled and ready to fire. The narrow corridor was empty. Tables had been overturned and a picture on the wall had been knocked to the floor. He raced forward, glanced into Audrey's room, and saw it was empty.

By the time he got to the front door, all that remained was a billowing dust cloud kicked up by galloping horses. Dennison had taken her. Slocum started for the back of the house where he'd left his mare, then stopped. There was something he had to take care of first. Something important.

16

Slocum knew he ought to get after Dennison as quickly as possible since he held Audrey prisoner. What Dennison and the men with him could do to her wasn't to be borne by any woman, living or dead. But there was time. A little. He had to see something for himself first. Slocum went to her bedroom and rummaged about under the bed until he found her case.

He pulled it up and dropped it onto the bed. He stared at the closed lid, wondering if he wanted to know what he would find there. After a few seconds, he knew he did. If he discovered a wanted poster with his picture on it, that meant Audrey had tried to sell him to Sheriff Narvaiz—and he would leave her with Dennison and the rest of the James Gang, in spite of what that would mean to her.

But if he didn't find the wanted poster . . .

He flipped open the top of the case and saw an inch thick sheaf of posters. Staring at him from the top was a poor likeness of Charlie Dennison. Slocum quickly riffled through the remaining posters and not a one had his face on it. That didn't mean she hadn't turned the wanted poster over to the sheriff, but when he had spied on her, he hadn't seen anything like that happen. Audrey had obviously kept the posters as befitting a bounty hunter. Or a woman who fancied herself a bounty hunter.

But did she have a wanted poster on him? The way she had spoken to the sheriff fit Slocum to a T. Then he laughed harshly when he realized it also described Charlie Dennison. Audrey didn't know his past well enough to be able to understand how much alike he and the man who fancied himself Jesse James's top gunman were.

Slocum closed the lid and stashed the case back under the bed. He hadn't satisfied his need to know what kind of a deal Audrey had with the sheriff, but he hadn't seen anything that told him she wanted a bounty on his head either.

Running out the back way, vaulting over the dead woman, and avoiding the pool of her blood, he got to his horse and hit the trail after Dennison and the others. He saw no reason for the kidnappers to leave town when it was solidly under Jesse's thumb now. But where would they take a lovely woman?

There was only one place. The Eagle Hotel was a three-story brick building and reputedly the most top-notch hotel this side of Taos. If Dennison wanted to have his way with Audrey, he'd do it in the finest surroundings possible.

He trotted through the smoke and debris as a couple of Jesse's gang waved to him. He acknowledged them but didn't stop to get sucked into a long conversation or self-congratulation on such a quick victory. In the plaza the soldiers rounded up the last of the townspeople fighting against Jesse. Slocum ignored them and saw four horses tethered outside the hotel.

That was the right number for Dennison, his two henchmen, and their captive.

Slocum hit the ground, lashed his reins around an iron ring set at the side of the hotel, and clomped up onto the boardwalk. The fancy etched glass door had been smashed, leaving shards on the floor that crunched under his boots. The faint smell of something burned made his nose twitch, but he ignored all this as he went to the room clerk, who cowered behind the desk.

"Where did they take her?"

The clerk turned even whiter and stammered out an answer Slocum couldn't understand. He reached across the counter and grabbed the front of the man's shirt and twisted, choking him. This produced the answer he needed.

"Th-Third floor. Presidential suite. They took a couple bottles of champagne, too."

Slocum released him, then drew his six-shooter. The clerk sobbed for mercy, but Slocum only wanted to be sure he carried six loaded chambers. Firing as he had during his meandering trip through Las Vegas, he had lost count. It was the work of a minute to be sure he was ready to face Dennison and his cronies. Taking the steps two at a time, he was on the third landing before he knew it.

One of the men stood outside the door, his ear pressed to the panel. He heard Slocum come up but didn't turn to see who joined him.

"Come on over and listen. This is just getting good."

He half turned when Slocum didn't immediately join him eavesdropping on the trio inside the room. The man's eyes widened and he went for his six-gun. Slocum swung his Colt and smashed the side of the man's head. From the way bone crunched and the man's head flopped about like a rag doll's, he wasn't going to be getting up ever again. Slocum picked up the outlaw's six-shooter. He had learned to never leave behind a weapon if he could use it—and he would be facing two armed and dangerous men inside.

Two of his guns against theirs. It seemed a good match.

Slocum kicked in the door so hard it slammed back against the wall and then rebounded, trying to close itself. In the instant it was open, but before it swung back, Slocum emptied the six-shooter he had taken from the fallen outlaw at the bare-assed man on the bed holding down Audrey Underwood.

The man shrieked in pain and flopped about. Slocum saw

at least two bullet holes in the man's rear end that would slow him down. In the room confusion reigned supreme. The wounded outlaw screamed, Audrey screamed, and Dennison barked out orders that did nothing but give away his location.

When Slocum kicked open the door the second time, he aimed his trusty Colt Navy at the corner where he'd heard Dennison. He fired twice and both rounds hit home. Charlie Dennison gasped and bent double.

On the bed Audrey struggled to pull up her torn clothing. Slocum ignored her and sought the man who had been ready to rape her. A bit of the man's bald head poked up over the far side of the bed. Two more quick shots ended the man's life. The first grazed his head and caused him to react by straightening, giving Slocum the target for a killing shot. The second slug hit the man in the middle of the forehead, killing him instantly.

"John, thank God. You—"

Slocum turned back to Dennison, who didn't have the good grace to die. He clutched his belly but was far from dead. He got off a round that forced Slocum to dodge. Slocum's boot tangled in the rug and sent him crashing to the floor, giving Dennison a second chance to kill him.

Slocum fired and his hammer fell on an empty chamber. He was out of ammo.

"I told Jesse he oughtta kill you, but he has some harebrained idea him and you rode together in the war, so you're one of us." Dennison took two steps forward. Sweat dripped from his pale face but there was a look of utter madness there that told Slocum his life was about ready to end. "I told him to kill you but he wouldn't. So I will. My pleasure to." Dennison lifted his gun to fire and found himself knocked back by a scratching, biting wildcat.

Slocum rolled around, got his feet under him, and dived into the pile, ripping Dennison's six-gun from his hand, then pushing Audrey back.

"I'll finish this."

Slocum swung a hard fist and knocked back Dennison's head, but the outlaw wasn't done yet. He stumbled to his feet and squared off. As Slocum came at him, he got in a punch. The hard blow to Slocum's belly slowed him, but he once had fought a hundred rounds in a bare-knuckle fight and won. A hundred knockdowns and all of them hadn't been his opponent—only the last one had left his opponent unable to rise for another round.

"I'm going to get real pleasure out of this," Slocum said, then he swung and missed. Dennison moved faster than a man with two slugs in his gut had any right to. As Slocum prepared to land another blow, a sharp report next to his ear momentarily deafened him. Then Dennison fell forward into his arms.

Slocum let him drop facedown to the floor and turned to a half-naked Audrey. She held Dennison's pistol in her hand.

"My bounty, not yours," she said in a quavering voice. He took the gun from her grip and tossed it onto the bed. She came into his arms and shivered, then finally pushed back and said, "I must get decent if I'm going to take his body to the sheriff and claim my reward."

"You don't know what's gone on in town, do you?" He explained how Jesse had finally launched his revolt and the outcome so far.

"He'll get himself killed, and I'll lose the reward," Audrey said. She pulled up her blouse and tried to straighten her skirt. The cloth was torn and the best she could do was tuck in parts to keep from being too exposed.

"I'll be sure the gang's still out riding around town," Slocum said sarcastically, "so you can go round them up for the sheriff."

"Do that, John. I'll be there in a minute. Oh!" She threw her hands up in exasperation as her blouse fell open in the front.

Slocum grinned.

"Nice view from here."

"Go, go. Hurry." He stepped out into the hall, then re-membered he had wanted to tell her to bring along Denni-son's pistol. He opened the door and stopped, intrigued by the way she rummaged through the dead outlaw's pockets. She found a scrap of paper and unfolded it. She held it up to get a better look at it, then refolded and tucked it away into the folds of her skirt. Only then did she go about mak-ing herself presentable in public.

Slocum waited a few seconds then made a big show of coming into the room. Audrey looked innocent as she sat on the bed, her blouse tied in the places where it had been ripped.

"Don't forget to bring his gun," he said, pointing to Den-nison. "All the ammo you can find, too. We might have to shoot our way out of town."

"We can't leave," she said. "This is where everything is happening. Jesse isn't going to run. He'll stay and—"

"Forget the reward on his head. Keeping your pretty head attached to your shoulders is more important. Write a newspaper article about it. You'll get paid for that."

"Five dollars," she said glumly. "The reward is ever so much bigger for Jesse James."

"What about him? Dennison ought to be worth something."

"A hundred dollars," she said without hesitation. "I have a wanted poster on him, but it wasn't dead or alive. Just alive."

"Thanks," Slocum said. She looked up at him, startled. "Thanks for deciding I was worth more than a hundred dollars."

"I wasn't aiming to kill him," she said, and Slocum couldn't tell if Audrey was joking. She hefted the gun, got to her feet, and motioned for him to get out into the hall.

Slocum ducked back into the corridor and ran to the land-ing. He motioned her back when he heard voices below. Angry voices. One might have been Frank James but he couldn't tell.

"That way," he said. He took her by the arm and hurried her along to a door leading out to stairs going to the alley behind the hotel.

"Where are we going?" Audrey tried to stop on the stairs but Slocum kept her moving. When the others in the gang found Charlie Dennison and the other two dead, all hell would be out for recess. Slocum wanted to be as far away as possible when that happened.

"You're returning to the boardinghouse, going to saddle your horse, and get out of Las Vegas. This is one dangerous place now." To underscore that, a bullet spanged against the wall and ricocheted when it hit a nail.

"All right," she said. "But how do I find you?"

"Why do you say that?"

"There's something in your tone that says you're not coming with me."

"I've got unfinished business," Slocum said, remembering how Sergeant Berglund had ordered him killed. This was the only chance he'd have to set things right.

"The gold, John, there's a mountain of gold out there and Jesse is going to squander it on buying merchants and soldiers and guns!"

"You'd prefer to take it before he spends it on someone else?"

"Exactly!"

"Get back to the boardinghouse and hightail it," he said. He slapped her on the ass. "And you have a very pretty tail, too."

She started to argue, then kissed him quickly and headed off. Slocum wondered what was on the paper she had taken from Dennison's pocket. It might have been the location of another gold hoard. Or it might be nothing at all. He didn't care if she found the gold and got away with it. That would put an end to Jesse's cockeyed rebellion plan faster than anything short of killing the outlaw.

He walked to the front of the hotel and glanced into the lobby. The clerk fearfully watched as several of Jesse's gang stood on the first landing, six-shooters ready for action. He didn't have to see them to know several others had pushed on up to the top floor and the presidential suite. By now they'd've found Dennison and the other two dead.

This was the perfect time to add to the number of those waiting to be buried. He had a beef to settle with Simon Berglund.

As Slocum stepped out into the street, he heard a bugle sound from south of town. He turned and saw the sergeant with his men in the plaza. Berglund reformed them and then they turned on any of Jesse's gang around them. Slocum lifted his pistol to fire but felt a sharp pain in his back.

"Got a bayonet ready to run you through. You just put that six-gun of yours away and march to the plaza."

Slocum looked over his shoulder. A soldier had him dead to rights. Worse, a second bluecoat stood a pace to the side. Even if Slocum batted away the bayonet and stayed clear of any shot, the second soldier would have him.

He thought it was strange that they didn't order him to throw away his gun, but he walked to the plaza, hands up. Berglund was busy with a half-dozen other outlaws, including Jesse James. It surprised Slocum that Berglund had been able to capture the notorious outlaw so easily. Even stranger, the sergeant hadn't killed him outright.

Berglund must want the hidden gold with a passion that knew no bounds and only Jesse could deliver its location.

Two companies of cavalry came trotting up. The horse soldiers had their carbines ready to fire, but there wasn't any opposition. Berglund had herded the gang into a tight knot in the plaza and had them surrounded by his company, all with bayonets fixed.

"Sergeant Berglund, report!" The captain at the head of the column stared at the dozen outlaws.

"These men were shooting up the town but my unit subdued them, sir."

"They did more than shoot up the place," the captain said, looking around. "They damned near burned Las Vegas to the ground!"

"We stopped 'em, sir, before they could do much more."

"Is this the lot of them?" The captain glared at Slocum and the others.

"You might have us cooped up, but we'll get away!" Jesse shouted.

"Yes, sir, the lot of them. That there's Jesse James himself." Berglund pointed at the outlaw with his pistol.

"Well done, Sergeant. Very well done. There will be a commendation for you. Move them out. Get them into the fort's stockade."

Slocum looked around and knew Frank James and the others that had rushed into the Eagle Hotel weren't captured. Berglund had to know that. And as the soldiers with the fixed bayonets moved them out onto the road leading toward the distant Fort Union, Slocum realized he still had his six-shooter at his hip. Jesse had a solitary six-shooter tucked into his belt and hidden by his vest and coat. The others were similarly armed with their guns hidden. Slocum took his from the holster and shoved it into his belt so he could keep it out of sight, too.

A soldier at his side watched and said nothing.

"We got their horses ready, Sergeant Berglund," a corporal called.

Slocum wanted to talk to Jesse, but the outlaw was busy whispering to the others in his gang—and to Berglund.

"Very good, Corporal. Get them mounted and back to the fort as quick as they can ride."

"Sarge, the captain's riding with us." The quaver of panic in the private's voice as he reported told Slocum something wasn't going according to plan.

"We'll escort you, Sergeant," the captain called. He arrayed his company ahead of Berglund's men and the prisoners.

Slocum heard Jesse James curse under his breath. Then they were on their horses and being herded toward Fort Union and the stockade, staring at the score of bluecoat soldiers ahead of them on the road.

17

"Post double guards on the prisoners, Sergeant." The captain sat on his horse, acting as if he posed for a statue. Slocum thought that might be running through the officer's mind since he would go down in history as the man who had finally captured Jesse James and the rest of his gang. The captain was so wrapped up in what he thought was a decisive victory that he never even looked at his prisoners to see if they were armed. He assumed they had been disarmed by his dutiful Sergeant Berglund.

Jesse and the gang now being crowded into the small stockade cells carried more firepower than the captain's entire company. None of the soldiers moving them into those cells paid the least attention to the butts of six-shooters poking out of belts or the knives and other weapons hidden on their prisoners. The payoff gold jingling in their pockets was almost palpable.

Prisoners, Slocum reflected, was hardly the right way to name those placed into the Fort Union stockade. And for all that, the soldiers weren't hardly bluecoats anymore. Whatever Berglund had promised them for getting Jesse and the

others into the fort walls turned them into traitors, not soldiers.

Even so, no matter the handful of turncoats in his command, the captain ought to have asked each prisoner his
name. He would have realized many—most—of the gang
had not been rounded up. Frank James was missing as were
others that had ridden into New Mexico Territory with Jesse.
Most of those now incarcerated were new recruits, not the
battle-hardened veterans from Missouri.

"You and you, stand guard outside," Berglund said, ordering two of his men to keep away anyone curious about
the notorious prisoners. When he was sure no one was likely
to eavesdrop, Berglund opened the cell doors himself. Slocum remained at the rear of one cell, letting three other outlaws block the sergeant's direct view of him. He might be
armed, but if the trooper spotted him, no amount of firepower was likely to stop Berglund from killing him.

"You can wait in here until the company's at mess,"
Berglund said.

"You have the keys to the armory?" Jesse strutted forward, the cock of the walk. And why not? He was getting
ready to take control of an entire U.S. Army post, and this
after he had seized control of Las Vegas. For him, it was a
day of victories that were only just beginning.

"I'll have them. I'm negotiating with the armorer. He's
willing but wants more gold." Berglund paused. "Just like
me and the boys here. We want to be sure we're getting
paid."

"I told you that Charlie Dennison has the map to your
gold. It's quite a mountain, too," Jesse said.

"I trust him, as much as I do any of you sons of bitches,"
Berglund said.

"Why shouldn't you? He's your cousin."

Slocum bit down on his lip to keep from saying anything
that would draw attention to him. He shifted his six-gun
from his belt to his holster, where it rested more comforta-

bly. Drawing a pistol thrust into his belt was far slower than clearing the leather of a holster. There wasn't as much chance of the hammer tangling in cloth either. Slocum had seen some men who preferred to carry their six-gun in their coat pocket, but the smartest, fastest, and likeliest of them to survive also lined the pocket with leather like a marshal he had seen in El Paso.

Jesse didn't know Dennison was dead, and neither did Berglund. And when Frank got around to letting them know, he'd also pass along that Dennison didn't have the map to the gold. How long would it be until someone figured out Audrey Underwood had it? Or was that even possible? Dennison might have taken a fancy to Audrey and decided to have at her surrounded by the luxury of the fancy hotel suite. The two gunmen with him were dead. It was possible nobody else in the gang had an inkling what Dennison had been up to or that he had been with Audrey when he died.

That meant Audrey might find the gold and clear out before Slocum could find her. At the moment, as appealing as the notion of more gold than his horse could carry was, getting away from the post without Berglund spotting him was more important. Shrouds didn't have pockets.

"He's my cousin but he's a double-dealing snake who rode with you damned rebels during the war," Berglund said. "How do I know he hasn't fetched the gold for himself?"

"Because," Jesse said with such confidence that Slocum almost believed him, "Charlie is not a stupid man. I've promised him a hundred times as much gold if he sticks with me. He speaks Spanish, so I reckon he was the obvious one to put in charge of Mexico after the Knights of the Golden Circle take over there."

"Him running an entire country?" Berglund laughed harshly. "It'd be something he would try, but he couldn't steal from the treasury fast enough before he had a line of men ready to shoot him."

Or women, Slocum silently added. For all Charlie Dennison's enemies, it had been a woman who had put a bullet through him, ending his foul life.

"You'd better report to the captain," Jesse said. "Or is the colonel back from patrol yet?"

"That worries me a mite," Berglund said. "Colonel Loebe has enough men to retake the fort if we can't get at least half the ones not already in my pocket to go along. He's been out tracking down a band of Comanches who bought themselves some rifles and are making a nuisance of themselves."

"Cannon," Jesse said, his assurance contagious. "And there's a Gatling or two in the armory. We let the colonel ride on in to the parade ground and turn him into mincemeat."

"Can't let him get away. Can't let any of them get to a telegraph. One wire back East and the whole damn Trans-Mississippi Army will be here in a week."

"I'm taking care of that," Jesse said.

Since the railroad went into Lamy, Slocum guessed the merchant he had seen Jesse paying off had something to do with either crippling the telegraph or passing along intelligence about troops being moved in by train. On horseback would be reasonable, but not if Sheridan thought a quick strike was preferable to a gradual escalation. From what Slocum knew of Sheridan, he would end up losing a couple companies of men rather than listen to Sherman, who would insist on sending enough men and supplies for a year-long siege.

That was the difference in the commanders, and it would work against Sheridan. By the time W. T. Sherman got his way with Grant, the Knights of the Golden Circle would be fortified and ready for war in their fledgling country.

"Just so you remember that you'll need me after you set your ass on that throne."

"Throne? Never," Jesse said, laughing. "I'm going to be the president of my own country. I don't hold with kings or *caudillos*."

"Just so you remember that," Simon Berglund said. He looked around the stockade, most of the men crowded into the small office and away from the cells, then took a deep breath, brushed trail dust off his uniform, and marched out to meet with the officers commanding the post.

If Jesse was smart, he'd have Berglund draw his pistol and shoot the officers. And Jesse James was nothing but clever when it came to such treachery. Slocum felt the pressure on him to get the hell out of Fort Union as fast as he could.

"The company's filing into the mess hall," Jesse said, peering out the partially opened door across the parade grounds. "Get ready, men. We're about to make history."

The outlaws around him murmured and moved toward the door, carrying Slocum along with them. He let them since he had to get out of the stockade anyway. Once outside he could find his horse and shoot his way out, if necessary. He guessed that when the bullets started flying, the guards on the walls would leave their posts to support their comrades inside the fort. Escaping then would be as simple as opening the gate.

Slocum hung back but ran into bad luck when Jesse spotted him.

"Slocum. Slocum! Come on up here. I got a special task for you. You're the best damned shot I ever saw. I want you to take out the sentry on the wall behind the armory."

"I can't do it with a pistol," Slocum complained. "I'll get my Winchester and—"

"Can't go to the stables. There's a dozen men bivouacked there. The barracks are overflowing, so they're putting troops up there. Don't worry your head about having a rifle. We'll find one along the way. A Spencer good enough for you?"

"Don't want a carbine. The barrel's too short for accurate shooting."

"I'll see what I can scare up."

The sun was dipping behind the mountains to the far west

and the mosquitoes from along the river were beginning to buzz. Slocum swatted a couple, then gave up. They'd have to drill through his tough hide if they wanted to suck out any of his blood, and he was more inclined to worry about bigger quantities of his precious blood being spilled by the likes of Jesse James—or Simon Berglund.

Slocum expected Jesse to go find a soldier who was going along with his scheme but he only motioned to one standing guard beside the stockade.

"Your rifle. Hand it over." The soldier hesitated. "Now, dammit. You want to hang for treason?" This produced a quick transfer of the rifle. Jesse tossed it to Slocum. "That ought to do you just fine."

"There?" Slocum pointed to a guard pacing along the low wall on the east side of the fort. The hulking, dark building a few yards from the wall had to be the armory.

"We'll get ready to go in, but you need to take him out before we break out the rifles."

Slocum walked toward the armory, not wanting to gun down the sentry but not seeing any way around it. If he failed, Jesse would kill him. Worse, if he didn't fail, he might bring down the rest of the soldiers busy chowing down in the mess hall. He'd wish then that Jesse had put a bullet in the back of his skull.

There was a scuffle ahead, then silence. Jesse pushed him forward.

"This is a good spot to get him," Jesse said.

"Looks like it," Slocum said. He made sure the cartridge was seated properly in the receiver, took off the bayonet so he could swing the barrel around more easily, then braced himself against the side of the armory and sighted in the sentry outlined against the twilight sky. From outside the man was protected by the waist-high wall but no one thought to guard the sentry from a shot fired at this angle.

Before Slocum could squeeze back on the trigger, a shout startled him.

"What's going on? Hey. Prisoners! Escape! The prisoners done escaped the stockade!"

Slocum turned, leveled his rifle, and fired at the soldier shouting the warning. The bullet must have sailed close to his head, because he ducked and ran back toward the mess hall, screeching like a stuck pig the whole way.

"Damnation, this is going to get difficult. Where's Berglund? We need some heavy firepower right now."

Slocum looked at the locks on the door. Shooting them off was out of the question. The heavy iron hasps and locking mechanism were designed to withstand anything short of a stick of dynamite. He used the butt end of the rifle and found that a sledgehammer was more likely to break the locks.

"Where's Berglund? Get his sorry ass over here right now!"

As Jesse issued his command, three shots came from the direction of the commander's office on the south side of the parade grounds. Then a fourth shot lit up the window. Sergeant Berglund stepped out, pistol in his hand.

He took in the commotion at the mess hall and rushed over there, bellowing orders as he went. Since no one else appeared to know what was happening, the soldiers listened to him. Slocum cursed his bad luck. If he had his wits about him after Berglund finished off the officers, he could have drilled him as he stepped out. That would have thrown the entire post into confusion.

"Good, good," Jesse said. "Berglund's taking control and we won't have to worry so much about killing the lot of them. This is working out better than I thought."

"His neck is in a noose now," Slocum said. "He gunned down the officers. You tell him to do that?"

"No, but it was a nice touch. I was planning on a firing squad for them to let the rest of the soldiers see what'd happen if they didn't throw in with us. That'd save having to buy the lot of them."

"There's only so much gold to go around," Slocum said dryly.

"All the more for me . . . and you, Slocum. For you, too. We're going to be rich and powerful."

"Santa Fe," he muttered.

"Yeah, you get Santa Fe."

"But Dennison is getting Mexico."

"Don't get greedy on me, Slocum. We're making good progress today toward having our own country. One step at a time. Now get that sentry taken out."

Slocum saw Berglund and a dozen soldiers coming toward them. He fingered the rifle and considered his chances of making a killing shot on the sergeant. Turning, he looked up at the sentry in time to see a foot-long orange flash from the soldier's muzzle. The bullet tore past Slocum and embedded in the armory wall. The man had figured out what was going on and had identified the source of danger to Fort Union.

Lifting his rifle, Slocum sighted in and fired in one smooth motion. The sentry yelped, dropped his rifle, and tumbled backward, falling over the low wall. A thud followed by a low moan told that the soldier was still alive but not likely to get in their hair.

"Should have killed him," Jesse complained. "You can do it later, when we get the rifles and all the rest inside." He pounded his fist against the armory.

"Where are your men, Jesse?" Berglund called. "This all of them?"

"You know it is. We need to get the rifles out of there fast."

"I ordered the men in the mess hall to finish eating. They won't bother us."

"Where're the keys to these locks? You'd think you had gold stored inside." Jesse rattled one lock. "Well? Open them."

"These are all your men, aren't they, Jesse?"

Slocum pressed himself against the back wall and faded into the shadows. He heard in Berglund's voice what Jesse James didn't.

"We got to hurry, dammit. The sooner we replace the guards with our men and have the cannon ready, your colonel can come back anytime he wants."

"No telling when Colonel Loebe will be back. Now, men, now!"

A ragged volley sounded and half of Jesse's gang died. Slocum dropped the rifle and started for the far side of the armory. His retreat was cut off by a soldier holding his rifle at port arms. Slocum froze. Movement would draw unwanted attention.

"What's going on, Berglund?" Jesse was outraged. "Why did you shoot my men? Put down your pistol!"

"You don't understand, do you? You whipped up a fine plan to set up your own country. I've been thinking on it and can't figure out one thing."

"What?" Jesse James was beginning to understand what had happened.

"Why do I need you? Why can't I be the one raking in the gold and ruling over an entire country? Fort Union controls the Santa Fe Trail, and as of right now, I'm in command of the fort!"

There was a meaty thud, and Jesse's outraged reply was cut off. Slocum pressed harder against the wall, hoping the shadow would cloak him from the soldier.

It didn't.

The bluecoat half turned, then took a couple steps toward Slocum, lowering his rifle as he prepared to shoot.

18

Slocum held his breath as the guard cautiously advanced. Then the soldier stopped, craned his neck around, and peered up at the armory roof before stepping out a few paces and aiming his rifle aloft.

"Get down or I'll shoot!" The soldier pulled back the hammer on his carbine. Slocum knew this was the only time he was likely to have a chance to get rid of the soldier and make a break for freedom. He remained stock-still, staring at his potential adversary. From above Slocum heard scraping on the roof.

"Halt! I'll fire!"

Then the soldier loosed a round that nicked the corner of the roof and brought down one of Jesse's gang, flailing and fluttering as if he was a bird with a broken wing. He crashed to the ground with a thud and a whoosh as air rushed from his lungs. Slocum finally caught a little luck. The outlaw had fallen away from where he stood, so the soldier pivoted, his back to Slocum, and aimed his rifle at his prisoner.

Again, Slocum could have acted. A quick swing of his pistol and he could connect with the back of the soldier's head. And again he remained frozen in shadows, heart hammering as the soldier poked the man on the ground.

"Get up. You ain't hurt. I missed you by a country mile."

The outlaw moaned and struggled to get his wind back. The soldier poked him again and this brought some life to the fallen man. He stumbled to his feet, still gasping for air, and let the soldier march him away from Slocum.

"Lookee what I got," the soldier called. Slocum saw two more soldiers come to the far end of the armory but they only had eyes for their prisoner, taking his six-shooter and shoving him back toward the parade ground. Slocum edged along the back of the armory and cautiously peered around the side. The three soldiers had more than a half-dozen men in their sights. Neither Simon Berglund nor Jesse James was anywhere to be seen.

Dropping to his belly, Slocum wiggled along the foundations until he had a clear look around the building to where Berglund held Jesse pinned against the wall with a bayonet shoved hard against his belly. For an instant he thought the sergeant had impaled Jesse, then he settled down when he saw the outlaw leader was still alive.

Alive and furious.

"You can't do this, Berglund. You can't switch sides!" Jesse cried.

"Not switching sides," Berglund said. "That'd mean I was sticking with being a soldier. You promised me gold and delivered a dollop or two, but you weren't in this for the gold. You wanted to rule over your own country."

"I want to get a new Confederacy started," Jesse said. "This time we'll stop 'em cold."

"No, you won't. You wanted power. With the power could come all the money you could spend. Why should I get your pickings? I want what you were after. I'm going to be the ruler of this here new country."

"I've got backers in Washington," Jesse said.

"Others in the Knights of the Golden Circle," Berglund

said, nodding. "Does it matter two hoots and a holler to them who's out here? I don't think so. I agree to go along with them, they'll back me just like they was backin' you." Berglund laughed and it was harsh and ugly. "I can have it all, Jesse. Turn in a notorious outlaw for the reward. What are you worth? Five hundred dollars?"

"More," Jesse said angrily. "You might kill me but my brother'll get you, Berglund. And if Frank doesn't, my cousins will. *Your* cousin will. Dennison is my man, *mine*! He knows which side of the bread his butter's on!"

"I have an entire army post at my command. Letting the soldiers know they have a new commander is going to be fun. I was a major before they busted me. I'll be a colonel this time. A general. And then a president!" Berglund laughed nastily. "And Charlie? He's going with whoever has the power. He wouldn't risk his precious neck to save you, not if it means he can still get whatever you promised him. I'll let him have it, Jesse. I'll give it all to him. Which of us do you think he'll back? You or a blood relative? Me!"

Jesse fell silent. Slocum knew what was going through the outlaw's head about now. He had plotted and planned, stolen and hoarded the gold to become undisputed ruler of a new country sliced from the edges of the hated U.S.A. Everything had gone well and he had seized not only a small town but Las Vegas and probably Santa Fe by now. He hadn't counted on a man with even more ambition and less honor coveting what he forged in the name of the Knights of the Golden Circle.

"Bugler, blow assembly!" Simon Berglund stepped back but kept the bayonet point pressed hard into Jesse's belly. The troops rushed out and formed ranks on the parade ground. Slocum lay still as some soldiers ran past him in the gathering darkness. They were too intent on what was happening, why their sergeant assembled them in the dark, a hundred other questions, and never spotted Slocum. He considered a single shot to take out Berglund, but Slocum couldn't see how that helped him get the hell off the post alive.

Berglund motioned for three privates behind him to guard Jesse while he strutted into the parade ground, as if he were the commander-in-chief and these were his personal guards. Slocum snorted at the idea that Berglund wasn't too far wrong.

"We have a great opportunity, men," Berglund bellowed. "These outlaws have killed our officers, leaving me the highest-ranking soldier at Fort Union. I am assuming command."

"Where's the colonel?" a soldier at the rear of the company called out.

"He is out fighting Comanches and won't return for some time."

Slocum heard the change in Berglund's tone and knew then that he wasn't going to offer these men what Jesse had offered his in return for their support. Too many of these soldiers were battle-hardened veterans of the war and loyal Federalists. Berglund would find himself a small number of soldiers willing to risk everything in a revolt. The rest would go along as dupes. Slocum knew full well how a post commander controlled the flow of news. Gossip abounded but a good officer used it to his own advantage.

Berglund would keep what was happening outside the fort a secret as he consolidated his power. At first it would be easy enough using the troops against Frank James and those still controlling Las Vegas. After he eliminated his rivals, Berglund had to recruit more of the soldiers to his side. But if he did so, he could spread his influence throughout northern New Mexico and finish the conquest Jesse had begun.

Jesse James's plan had been good. Control the railroad and prevent immediate troop movement. By the time cavalry was brought in on horseback from nearby forts, he would have complete control of the civilian population and be able to repulse a counterattack. With his allies in Washington and possibly in the War Department, Jesse could have made it work.

Berglund had to find out who those men in power were and ally himself. But if he kept control of Fort Union, he held an ace in the hole. Since Jesse had intended for Berglund to be the one at the head of the Army unit turned against the U.S.A., this was simple enough. Jesse just hadn't considered power meant more to a former officer than gold. Old habits of command died a slow death in any officer reduced in rank to noncom.

"We will lock up this fort as tight as a drum. We will zealously guard the prisoners we have taken. And then at first light, we will form an attack force and drive out the outlaws still controlling Las Vegas and place the town under martial law."

A cheer went up, though many of the gathered soldiers weren't sure what they cheered. Berglund dismissed them and came back to where Jesse was closely guarded.

"You heard that, didn't you?" Berglund asked. "I'll rout your brother and the rest of the gang, find those you have installed as your civilian puppets, and then proceed to cast my net even wider."

"The colonel is still in the field. How are you going to explain all this to him when he returns?"

"He might be killed by the Comanche. They are far better fighters than the men with him. If he isn't killed, I'll find a way to deal with him when he returns. He won't expect a squad of his own men to approach and cut him down, after all. I don't foresee trouble there. What I want from you is the location of your gold. All of it, not just the picayune amount you pledged to Charlie."

"Burn in hell," Jesse said, venom dripping from every word.

"I am sure that I will, but you will be there before me.

I'm not going to argue or wheedle. Tell me." Berglund waited and got no response. "Very well. I need to know your preference."

"What are you talking about?" Jesse tried to grab Berglund but the guards forced him back against the armory wall.

"It is quite simple. Do you want to be hanged at dawn or face a firing squad?"

Slocum couldn't hear what Jesse said, but it brought a short, barking laugh to Berglund's lips.

"Get him to the stockade, him and his other men. Keep a close guard on them or you'll be the ones standing in front of a firing squad alongside them."

Berglund did a smart about-face, then marched toward the commander's office. Slocum pressed himself flat into the ground as Berglund passed him. He could have reached out and tripped the sergeant, but Slocum needed to see how well disciplined the soldiers were. The detail marching Jesse and the remaining members of his gang back to the cells looked precise and were performing their duty with military precision.

On the main gate he saw four soldiers begin walking their posts. Escaping that way wasn't in the cards. There had to be another gate from the fort since it was so large and acted as a supply center. Slocum knew he could find it and slip through, but he wanted his horse under him when he did.

Before that, he had some scouting to do. Berglund wouldn't miss him among the prisoners being locked up since he hadn't identified him when they had been rounded up in Las Vegas for the mock arrest intended to lull the soldiers not going along with the plan into believing all was well. Moving from building to building, Slocum kept under cover until he came to the now deserted mess hall. The smell of food was more than he could resist.

Dangerous as it was, he stepped inside, took a tin plate,

and slopped out some of the stew. He added a hunk of hard-tack to sop up the gravy, found himself a spoon, and started to go find a hiding place outside to eat when a sharp command froze him in his tracks.

"Where you goin'? You know you ain't supposed to eat outside the mess hall."

"Taking it to Sergeant Berglund," Slocum said.

"Let the annoying little son of a bitch get his own food."

"He's in command of the whole damned post. Watch your tongue, Cookie."

"Don't call me that, you flat-footed cracker ass."

"You want me to tell him to fetch his own food?" Slocum still didn't turn.

"You ain't in uniform."

"That's because I'm a scout. The colonel didn't take all of us when he decided to go after that Comanche war party."

"Get the hell out of my mess hall. And bring back that plate all clean and shiny. I ain't washin' it for the likes of you or Sergeant Berglund."

Slocum stepped outside and let the rapidly cooling air soothe him. He had kept from having to kill the mess sergeant. The fewer bodies he left behind, the less likely he was to be found until he could figure out what had to be done.

He sank down behind the commanding officer's office, his back to the wall, and ate slowly. The stew tasted terrible, the meat was tough and needed salt. He sopped up all the gravy with the hard biscuit and then licked the plate clean. It was the first food he'd had in since he couldn't remember when. Belly full and no longer grumbling, he leaned back and closed his eyes, thinking on what was necessary. The jumble slowly straightened itself out and he didn't much like his conclusions.

For two cents he ought to let Jesse swing in the morning, but he needed the outlaw and the few of his remaining gang to get off the post. From everything he had seen, Berglund ran a well-disciplined force. The men might not like him but there was no reason for them to. The ones who would remain loyal to their rightful superiors weren't going to put up any kind of a fight—not yet. They might when they realized Berglund's real plans for them and for the territory they were ordered to defend. By then, it would be too late for Slocum to do more than join Jesse James in a shallow grave out behind the fort walls.

He pushed to his feet and studied the blank wall. He pressed his ear against the wood but heard nothing inside. Prying loose some of the mud used to chink up the holes between planks, he got a look into the office. Twisting around, he thought he saw most of the room. Empty. On the desk were spread maps and to one side a tin cup sent tiny curls of steam into the air. Berglund had been drinking coffee only a few minutes ago while he studied the maps.

Slocum found he had a real yen to study those maps, too.

He made his way along the back wall of several offices pressed together, took a quick peek around, and saw no one. Quick steps brought him to the boardwalk in front of the office doors. Out on the parade ground he saw Berglund waving his arms around and yelling about faulty protection on the fort walls. If Slocum was going to get into the office, he had to move fast.

His boots clacked and creaked on the old wood flooring as he stepped over the bloodstained section and hurried to get a look at the map spread across the desk. At first he couldn't make heads or tails of it, then he found a few landmarks and saw that Berglund had marked the cave where Jesse had placed the Knights of the Golden Circle symbols. Two other spots carried X's and then there were tiny dots showing supply lines and a large circle to the southeast, toward the Texas Panhandle. The dates inscribed in the circle told that this had to be the colonel's destination and times of patrol.

He looked up when he heard Berglund returning. Slocum's hand flew to his six-shooter and then he realized he was out of luck. Two soldiers came with Berglund, and from what he overheard, they were in cahoots with the sergeant, ready to carve out governorships for themselves in the new country.

He spun, pressed himself flat against the wall behind the door, and waited. The footsteps halted just outside. Slocum chanced a look between the door and the frame as Berglund stood with his hand on the latch, turned toward the men. Slocum started to poke his pistol through and get a shot off at Berglund when the man cursed, then pulled the door shut, and walked off.

Slocum opened the door a fraction and saw the sergeant with the two soldiers heading toward the main gate. Some problem had arisen that the new post commander needed to examine personally.

Trying to stay in shadows, Slocum left the office and hurried back toward the armory, making his way around the perimeter of the fort to reach the stockade. Berglund had ordered extra guards posted and he had gotten them. The men, usually standing solitary watch, stood in pairs. To get through the four men outside the stockade would require some mighty fancy shooting—and that would alert the rest of the post immediately.

A quick look through a slit window showed him two more soldiers stationed inside. Even if he had the best luck in the world, he couldn't hope to take out six soldiers with one shot each, get the cell doors open, and escape before every rifle in the fort was pointed at him.

Slocum went directly to the stable and got his horse as well as Jesse's and four others. He led them out onto the parade ground, bold as brass. If he had tried to sneak around, he would have been noticed. As it was, he was just another soldier hot-walking horses. He took a circuitous route and finally tethered the horses behind the stockade, hoping they didn't make too much noise and draw the attention of the guards.

He had one last stop to make. He went to the mess hall and found the buckets of grease outside the back door. He kicked them over, spattering the grease all over the wooden walls. Wishing he had more but knowing he didn't have time to hunt, Slocum took out a lucifer, lit it, and tossed it into the grease. The match sputtered fitfully, then found the grease and wood worth devouring. As the flames began licking up the back wall of the mess hall, he lit out running. He barely reached the stockade by the time the flames jumped higher than the mess hall roof and others took notice.

"Fire!" The cry went up and alarm bells sounded. As he had hoped, the four guards outside ran to help put out the fire. Slocum stepped into the stockade, six-shooter drawn. The two soldiers inside had been playing a game of gin rummy and had their hands on the table, not on their weapons.

"Keys," he snapped. "Where's the key ring?"

One soldier's eyes darted to the left. Slocum didn't let the muzzle of his pistol waver an inch as he stepped over and began fumbling about until he found the keys hanging on a peg.

"On your feet and into the cell block." One soldier started for his rifle but Slocum cocked his Colt Navy and the man turned into a pale, shaking statue. He read death in Slocum's eyes if he made any further move.

The two of them sidled backward.

"Jesse," Slocum called. "Where do they have you penned up?"

"Slocum? That you, Slocum?"

Slocum tossed the keys to the outlaw. When Jesse had freed himself and the others, Slocum herded the guards into an empty cell and kicked shut the door.

"Lock 'em up."

"Kill them, Slocum. I want to—"

Slocum slammed him hard against the bars.

"We don't have time. Nobody'll hear them over the ruckus I caused."

"I heard fire bells and smelled smoke. What'd you do, set fire to the whole damn fort?"

"I figured a pig roast was better than a neck stretching," Slocum said, herding Jesse James and the other outlaws from the room. "I've got horses out back. The only way we're going to get out is to ride like the wind for the gate. No shooting until we get close, then open up with everything we've got."

"We've done that before, haven't we, Slocum?"

Not answering, Slocum went out fast and circled the stockade. As he started to mount, sudden sharp pain blasted through his head. He sank to the ground.

"Reckon that makes us even for the time you buffaloed me."

Through blurred eyes and a red haze of pain, Slocum saw Jesse and the others mount and light out for the main gate at a dead gallop.

19

Head about to split apart, Slocum pulled himself up and onto his horse, but he was too woozy to ride. He heard distant gunfire and knew the James Gang was busting out of the fort. If Jesse made it, this would be yet another story to tell around the campfire. Such tales made the outlaw out to be something more than human, hardly a wisp of fog slipping through the fingers of lawmen everywhere. As Slocum regained his senses, he vowed to put an end to the desperado's life if he ever got the chance. He hadn't liked him when he rode with Quantrill and he liked him even less now that he had tried to leave him as a sop for Simon Berglund.

The sergeant would need a scapegoat, and Jesse had provided him one in John Slocum. A good hanging would go a ways toward reinforcing discipline and letting his troopers know he was truly in command. He might even hang the two soldiers locked up inside the stockade as a lesson for the others, though Slocum figured, through a head now only aching, that Berglund would be smarter to leave them locked up for thirty days for dereliction of duty. That would go a way farther as an object lesson than giving them a necktie party or even five lashes.

Slocum moved his bandanna around when it began to chafe—or he thought it did. He knew he was letting the scarf mimic a noose.

He shook his head, regretted it, and then focused his eyes on his saddle horn. When he had that right, he lifted his gaze and saw that the mess hall fire was almost extinguished. That meant he had little time to hightail it since there wasn't any more gunfire from the direction of the main gate. Either Jesse had escaped—again—or he lay dead on the ground. Either way, that gate was sealed to Slocum.

But he hadn't intended to leave Fort Union by the main gate. There had to be a postern somewhere around the wall. The details sent out to fetch firewood or water wouldn't always go through the main gate. Supplies might also be moved through a smaller gate. From what Slocum had seen of the fort's layout, the best place for such a small gate lay off on the far wall away from the stockade, out near the ice house at the far side of the corrals. He wanted to gallop off and find the gate, but he kept his horse moving at a deliberate pace. That had worked before when he had walked all the horses right past the noses of the soldiers.

"Halt, who goes there!" came the question as Slocum rode to a dark spot on the back wall. A sentry stepped out and was momentarily limned by the dying light from the distant fire.

"Got a mission from Sergeant Berglund," Slocum said. "A message that's got to reach the colonel right away."

"I ain't seen you around here before."

"I'm a scout just hired on. This is real important, so let me out."

"I need orders from Sergeant Berglund to—"

This was as far as Slocum let the private get before kicking out and catching him smack under the chin with the toe of his boot. The soldier's head snapped back, and he stumbled and fell hard against the wall. He might have busted his skull on the adobe bricks, but it didn't matter to Slocum. He rode closer, lifted the locking bar, and dropped it. Seconds later he had pushed the gate open far enough to squeeze through.

His eyes didn't focus quite right yet, but he got a sighting on the Big Dipper when clouds pulled free in the northern sky. The cold night air and the sense that he might have an entire company of cavalry on his trail kept him moving. His head cleared as he rode and just before dawn he trotted into Las Vegas. The town was silent and not what he expected from Frank James being in charge. Slocum rode to the marshal's office and saw a light burning inside. The office door stood ajar and he caught sight of Sheriff Narvaiz.

Slocum dismounted and went to the door. As softly as he walked, the sheriff looked up.

"What can I do for you?"

"You rounded up the outlaws?" Slocum asked. "The town's mighty quiet."

"We got some problems after Marshal Hooker was gunned down. Most of the fuss was raised by cavalry from over at the fort. I need to see what's going on. Got a half-dozen soldiers locked up, if you want to call them outlaws." Narvaiz frowned as he stared hard at Slocum, trying to remember where he had seen him. Slocum didn't want that thought finding an answer.

Slocum suspected Frank James and the rest had retreated from town when they learned that Jesse had been taken prisoner—or maybe Jesse had returned and realized his harebrained scheme was falling apart and the gang ought to get back to Missouri.

"I thought you'd want to know that there's some problem at the fort. Mutiny, but the commanding officer's on his way back from patrol. You might alert Colonel Loebe and let him take care of his problem. Just don't let him ride into the fort thinking he's still in command."

"Me and the colonel don't step on each other's toes," Narvaiz said, rubbing his chin. "That'd be the end of his career if word got out he had a mutiny." He looked over his shoulder in the direction of the cells where he had some of Berglund's men locked up. "Explains most all that's gone on in the past day or two here in town."

"Glad peace has been restored," Slocum said, stepping back. He started for his six-shooter when Narvaiz called after him but he didn't draw. A soldier had started cater-wauling and took the sheriff's attention away. Slocum hastily mounted and rode from town, going north, following the pole star.

As he rode, he thought on the map he had seen spread out on Berglund's desk. He got his bearings and cut across country, making his way higher into the hills. The one cave where Jesse had left all the ciphers wasn't likely anywhere the outlaw had stashed the gold again, but a second marked spot wasn't more than a mile farther along the ridge line. After an hour of picking his way through the rocky terrain and feeling warmed by the minute because of the spring sun on his back, Slocum heard sounds ahead on the game trail he followed.

"Damn it, Frank, how could that little shit have found the gold?"

"Don't ask me. I wasn't the one who trusted him."

"I didn't trust him," Jesse James shouted. "I was *using* him. He just beat me to the gun. Never thought he'd like my ideas so much he'd steal them."

"He stole more 'n your ideas, Jesse," Frank James said. "He stole our gold. What are we going to do?"

"Better tell the Knights that provided most of the gold," Jesse said, his voice crackling with anger. "I swear, I'll lead a damned army back and kill him myself."

"The way the sheriff moved into Las Vegas and rounded

up the soldiers tells me Berglund isn't going to be around that long. Narvaiz ain't nobody's fool and won't make mistakes now that he's seen what can go wrong."

Slocum rode closer, drew his six-shooter, and saw a small clearing ahead where Frank and Jesse stood almost nose to nose. None of the others from the gang were around, though Slocum took a quick look higher in the rocks to make sure Jesse hadn't posted lookouts. The best he could tell, the James brothers were the only other ones ahead.

"We're gonna look plumb stupid, Jesse, if any of this gets out."

"Doesn't have to," the outlaw said thoughtfully. "We told everybody we were leaving Missouri for a spell to let the law simmer down. It's been a month or so. If we go back, folks'll think those federal marshals aren't hunting for us anymore. Why tell them anything different?"

"The rest of the gang's not going to say anything since they're family. But the gold . . ."

Jesse and Frank mounted and rode east arguing about how they would spin the lie about their time in New Mexico and what they'd tell the Knights of the Golden Circle about how they'd lost so much gold. Slocum waited ten minutes until he knew they were gone to meet up with the survivors in the gang and hit the trail for Missouri.

Then he rode into the clearing and looked around. A smile came to his lips. A cave nestled up against the side of a steep hill drew him like a magnet does iron. He dismounted, went inside, and found the spot where a heavy box had been stored. From the depth in the soft earth, there might have been fifty pounds or so.

Gold. Fifty pounds of gold. That could mean as much as fifteen thousand dollars of the precious metal.

Slocum stepped out into the spring sun, then began a thorough examination of the ground. Frank and Jesse obviously had only arrived, found the gold missing, and thought Berglund had taken it since Frank would have informed

Jesse that Dennison was dead. Slocum led his horse along a path that meandered back around the hill toward the higher Sangre de Cristos and a watering hole. He tethered his mare a ways from the pool, then found himself a rock overlooking the water where he could sun himself. He drifted to sleep but came alert an hour later when he heard splashing.

He sat up and got a gander at a naked Audrey Underwood bathing in the pool. There was no reason for him to rush so he sat and enjoyed the view. Her long, slim legs were a wonder to behold, and as she turned, her bare breasts shone like alabaster in the hot New Mexico sun. She ran her hands over her sleek skin, scraping off dirt and enjoying the sensuous feel of being naked in a pool of water.

Slocum had to admit the water looked mighty inviting, with or without a naked Audrey Underwood in it.

When he had enjoyed the sights as much as possible, he slipped down the rock and walked to the pool. She spotted him coming and let out a squeal, then turned and faced him, standing waist deep in the water. She wrapped her arms around herself to hide her nakedness, then smiled and lowered her arms to her side so he got a full view of her loveliness.

"You're a mighty pretty sight."

"Been watching for very long? Oh, I know you, John. How long? How long have you been watching me do this?" She ran her hands over her wet breasts, caught the nipples, and tweaked them until the nubs were hard with desire as well as cold. "Or this?" Her slender hands stroked down over her belly, went lower, and vanished underwater. She closed her eyes and sighed. He felt himself responding. Something more than her finger ought to be exploring the delights hidden by the water.

He didn't protest when she stopped fingering herself and splashed closer, reaching up to begin unbuttoning his fly. His manhood jumped out, standing at attention from her careful ministrations.

"I've missed you, too, John. And this."

He began shucking off his shirt and kicked free of his boots as she pressed her mouth to him.

"That feels mighty good."

"I can make everything feel better," she said, flopping onto her back and splashing about in wanton invitation. Her fine legs, the auburn thatch between them, her breasts creating the ripples going from one side of the pool to the other— Slocum took it all in with a single glimpse, then moved into the water to join her. There was a time for watching and a time for doing.

"Let's see what we can do for each other," he said, stripping off the last of his clothes and swimming to the middle of the pool. Her naked flesh rubbed against his and he moved closer, drifting into the vee of her parted legs. She gasped as he entered her.

"Oh, so nice, John. I never thought I'd feel you in me again."

"You should have known you would," he said, kissing lightly at her damp bare flesh. "I saw you take the map from Charlie Dennison after you shot him. It led you to the gold."

"You knew all the time!"

"I knew I'd catch up with you after I took care of a small problem." He rotated his hips to stir his meaty length about inside her until they both gasped.

"No small problems here," she said, wiggling back and forth and pressing herself closer to his groin.

"How much? How much gold? I think it's around fifty pounds. You had to be pretty strong to lift that crate."

"I needed to keep my strength up for you, John. And for this." She kissed him hard and they began splashing about in the pool with greater purpose.

Slocum couldn't imagine a better way to get ready to spend a passel of gold.

Watch for

SLOCUM AND THE TRAIL TO TASCOSA

383rd novel in the exciting SLOCUM series
from Jove

Coming in January!